The Way Station

Cameron Black knows that it is time to pack away his guns. He and Virginia need to put their past behind them and when Cameron accepts a job running a quiet way station in the desert, it seems like the perfect way to forget old enemies.

But Cameron soon realizes it is never that easy to leave trouble behind. A stagecoach arrives at the way station. On it is an outlaw smuggling fifty thousand in gold and a young woman named Becky Grant, who is on the run from a rejected suitor. On their trail is Sheriff Beaton, Becky's wide-eyed suitor and rival bandits in pursuit of treasure.

Now, as a menacing dust storm gathers that threatens to keep them captive in the way station, Cameron Black knows he must use his guns once more. . . .

The Way Station

Owen G. Irons

A Black Horse Western

ROBERT HALE · LONDON

© Owen G. Irons 2011
First published in Great Britain 2011

ISBN 978-0-7090-9084-7

Robert Hale Limited
Clerkenwell House
Clerkenwell Green
London EC1R 0HT

www.halebooks.com

Typeset by
Derck Doyle & Associates, Shaw Heath
Printed and bound in Great Britain by
CPI Antony Rowe, Chippenham and Eastbourne

ONE

In the coolness of early dawn Cameron Black stepped outside of the way station and studied the long land, the garishly colored desert sky. It was a primitive place to make your last stand, but that was what he and Virginia had chosen to do. Finish up their long, troubled careers in the virtual isolation of the desert. A few doves had already taken to wing, flying toward water holes hidden among the stone-flanked hills. A coyote glanced at Cameron and slunk away furtively. A tangle of fifteen-foot high ocotillo plants, now flowering at their tips, cut dark, thorny silhouettes against the sky which had gone from gray to crimson to gold-limned blue and soon would become a white vault above them.

Whitey Carroll, who had arrived three months before from parts unknown, was already at work cutting wood for the kitchen stove which had to be kept burning so that six meals a day could be prepared – for the westbound stagecoach, for the passengers on the eastbound and, of course for the station crew. There was no way around that although during the summer the kitchen was a furnace. But then by noon on an August day, Borrego Springs was a furnace outdoors as well as in. Lucia, the young cook would already be up, muttering small Spanish curses as she banged iron kettles and copper pots around, a lot of the action unnecessary as Cameron knew. The woman had to protest her condition in some way. Cameron tried to keep his visits to Lucia's sanctum to a minimum. If there were any problems, Virginia would see to them. Her manner was more soothing.

Passing the corral, Cameron looked over the coach horses. They were still frisky at this time of the day; later a slow torpor would settle over them, only the twitching of their tails to chase away the horseflies indicating that they were alert in any way – and a part of that was probably reflex. They had plenty of hay and enough water – Cameron would have to tell Whitey to fill up the trough again when he was finished with his wood cutting.

The kid never objected to any job he was assigned, although he moved with painful slowness. Cameron could never tell if the young man was sun-struck or simply none too bright. Nevertheless, Whitey did all that was required of him and he would not be easy to replace out here on the empty land.

Cameron entered the dry shade of the barn. In the loft Archie Tate would still be sleeping until the heat awakened him later in the day. Tate was the hostler, and the wiry, bearded man seemed to have an internal clock which awakened him fully when it was time for an incoming stage. Then he was quick with his movements, unharnessing, hitching a fresh team with rapid skill. The rest of the time he lazed the days away in whatever shade he could find. He, too, did all that was required of him, and he, too, would not be easy to replace out on the desert. Both men were trustworthy in their own ways, and Cameron seldom interfered with their ideas of what their jobs entailed.

Having made his brief tour of the yard, Cameron returned to the way station's office where Virginia was already going over their tally books, making up a list of supplies they were running low on to send to the head office in Santa Fe. She looked sleepy to him, but not tired, really. Her gray-streaked dark hair was tied back loosely. She had a cup of coffee at her elbow.

7

'Hello, Scopes,' Cameron Black said, entering the room which was still cool thanks to its thick adobe walls. Virginia smiled.

It was an old joke, greeting her that way. Her name now, of course was Virginia Black, but when Cameron had first known her it had been Virginia Scopes. And when he had grown angry with her for small crimes, instead of calling her 'Ginnie' as he had when they were both much younger, he had taken to calling her Scopes.

If Borrego Springs might seem to be a kind of a hellish life to others, they had already been through several kinds of hell along life's trail, and this wilderness living was a kind of comfortable solitude to them at this point in their lives.

'Could you ask Lucia how we're doing with beans and rice? How many sacks we need for next month?' Virginia asked, turning her young-old eyes toward her husband.

'You want me to enter her kitchen?' Cameron asked with mock horror which caused Virginia's mouth to twitch into a smile.

'You can't be that afraid of her,' Virginia coaxed. 'A grown-up man like you?'

'She's already banging pots and pans around and the sun's barely risen.'

'I'm not asking you to move in with her,'

Virginia said. 'Just ask her how we're doing with beans and rice.'

'If I have to,' Cameron replied and Virginia's smile deepened. He kissed his recent bride and started toward the kitchen. Virginia watched him go: once one of the most feared gunmen in the territory afraid of a tiny Spanish cook! She knew he was mostly kidding with her, but also that he felt uneasy about confronting any of their employees. Things were just fine the way they were; he didn't want to disturb anyone, step on any toes.

She had met Cam so long ago that it did not seem possible that so many years had passed. As a girl she had admired the young gunfighter, cocky and sure of himself, his two guns worn low, his shoulders heavy with muscle, his dark curly hair always uncombed. She had seen Cameron take out two members of the Carson Plenty gang with a total of three shots. Her heart had fluttered with fear and pride at once.

Later the guns became too much for her. Cameron accepted all sorts of jobs, which he approached recklessly, returning to her only when he was exhausted or wounded. It was too much for a girl of her age to bear. Going to sleep at night, wondering where he was; waking in the morning wondering if he were dead. One morning when she felt that she could take no more, she had simply packed her bags and left.

He had drifted; she had drifted. Virginia had begun working in a dancehall and eventually turned to more profitable and dubious enterprises. When she had again met Cameron Black, twenty years on, she was besieged in an army outpost surrounded by Indians with her caravan of three camp-follower girls. That was when he had started calling her 'Scopes.' Debilitated so that he could no longer even draw his left-hand pistol, Cameron Black had nevertheless pulled them all out of a very dangerous situation.*

They had had a long ride to Santa Fe to discuss their past and their future. Neither was sure there could be another chance for them or where to even try it. They could not get past their mutual feelings of abandonment and blame, but they decided to go on with life. Cameron had landed a job with the stage company – one which no one else wanted – managing the way station at Borrego Springs and here they had landed, a tired former whore and an ex-gunfighter. They still had not worked out all of their problems, but they had married and come to Borrego, sure of one thing –

* *The Outpost* – Black Horse Westerns.

their troubled past could not follow them there.

At least that was their constant hope. The long desert, barren and blank, was their final refuge, their final home. Virginia sighed and got back to the books.

Cameron found himself hesitating at the kitchen door as another pan clattered to the floor. Lucia was in a mood today. He grinned, reminding himself of the times he had not flinched at stepping into a room to face half a dozen gunmen . . . all those years ago . . . and swung the door open to find Lucia, frozen in motion with another pot held high over her head. Her dark eyes sparked, her full lips twitched, but she said nothing and slowly lowered the pot.

Lucia was young still, slender, usually friendly, but mercurial.

'What's the trouble, Lucia?' Cam asked.

'Always the same trouble!' she spat. 'Where is Renaldo? He does not come for me. He left to go off to make money for us so that I could be his wife and not a cook-slave.' Her eyes suddenly moistened, and she sagged onto a straight-backed wooden chair, bowing her head. 'I am stuck here,' she murmured, 'and he is off riding, I do not know where.'

'I understand, Lucia,' Cameron Black said.

Whether the girl believed him or not, he really did. 'All you can do is be patient. Remember, Renaldo misses you as much as you miss him. He will return.'

Lucia dabbed at her eyes with her apron and nodded her head. 'Thank you, Señor Black,' she snuffled.

Cameron was briefly embarrassed by the gratitude in her eyes. 'Talk to Virginia after a while. She can probably give you better advice than I can. For now, will you check the larder and tell me how many more sacks of beans and rice you need for next month? Virginia says the list has to be sent to Santa Fe today on the eastbound stage.'

Returning to the office he found Virginia more alert, her hair brushed and pinned. She swiveled toward him in her chair.

'Lucia sounds more subdued,' Virginia said. 'What was it?'

'Renaldo again.'

'Oh! Whatever happened to that vaquero of hers, Cam?'

'I couldn't guess. I never knew the kid. I just hope he's managed to keep himself alive – for her sake.' He handed Virginia the list of items Lucia wanted from Santa Fe – she had added a few of her own. 'I told her to talk to you later . . . about times

12

like this,' Cameron Black said.

'Thanks,' Virginia said in a half-teasing tone.

'What else was I to do? I thought you could tell her that she's not the only one who's ever had this happen . . . waiting, I mean.'

'I know what you meant,' Virginia said. She rose to her feet and went to him, kissing him fully but not heavily. Holding Cam at arm's length, she asked, 'What are you going to do today?'

'I thought I'd better go out after a deer. We're down to four steers in the pen, and I don't expect them to drive a herd in from Santa Fe anytime soon.'

'No.' Virginia cocked her head. 'But you'd better wait awhile. Archie Tate is up and moving – what time is it?'

'Just about time for the westbound – but it's a little early.'

'You know Archie. If he's stirring, we've got a coach arriving.'

'I'll go and see if I can help him,' Cameron Black said. He crossed the room, paused at the door and turned back toward her. 'Virginia? Is this going to work out?'

'It has to, Cam. Damnit, it just has to. There are so few trails left for us to travel.'

Black locked eyes with her for a minute,

13

manufactured a smile, and went out into the heat and glare of the desert day.

Far out on the desert a plume of white dust could be seen rising into the pale skies. Archie Tate, seemingly alert now, was in the horse pen, selecting his four-horse team in a manner known only to him. These, the freshest, would be fitted into the coach harnesses as the used horses were hied into the corral for their rest.

'Going to need any help, Archie?' Cameron asked, approaching the corral. He placed his boot up on the lowest rail and squinted into the sun.

'Do I ever?' Archie asked, not sharply, but as if it were a slight slur on his ability. 'Better fill these troughs, though. Those are going to be some thirsty ponies arriving.'

'Didn't Whitey do that yet?' Cameron growled. Obviously the kid had not, and so Cameron busied himself with two pails, drawing water from the pump in the yard and carrying it back to the corral. By the time he was finished the coach was near enough to have form. It seemed to be Kyle Melrose driving. The narrow man with the long mustache was due, he supposed – Cameron had never taken the time to figure out the drivers' schedules. It was of little importance. The man beside Kyle in the box Cameron did not recognize

14

at all, but then the company was always hiring new shotgun riders. It wasn't only the danger of the job that drove off some of their best men, but the sheer boredom and discomfort that came with the job – riding on a rocking, jouncing stage for eight or twelve hours a day, during most of which nothing at all happened. By the end of the first shift the man would have heard all of the driver's tales and told most of his own. After that it was a heated ride across featureless land, your butt taking a beating from the hard wooden seat.

A lot of the shotgun riders went back to the job of working cattle which they had deserted, vainly looking for easier wages.

As Cameron knew, the shotgun riders could not be eternally vigilant. The sun had a way of causing a man to tug his hat low and sometimes to close his eyes. Then, when he least expected it, the coach might be hit by a gang of hold-up men with no compunction about shooting him dead. It was one of those jobs that looked romantic and interesting only to outsiders.

'Hold up there!' they heard Kyle Melrose shouting to his team of horses as he held back the reins. His face was grim. That, too, was not as easy as it seemed, holding back a team of four horses on the run, although most drivers slowed them to a walk

15

a mile or so out of the way stations to make the halting of the team easier. Some of these horses were only half-broken to the harness, well-trained animals being hard to come by on the desert.

Kyle brought the stage to a halt, cursed the horses, set the brake and climbed down heavily, rubbing his legs.

'Hello, Mr Black,' he said as Archie Tate moved in, ready to unhitch the well-used horses.

'Any trouble on the trail?' Cameron asked.

'No, thank God. But on some of these days I almost wish something would happen to enliven the run.'

'Don't wish anything like that on yourself.'

'I don't, really. One thing about these flat-desert runs is there's not a bush or a rock to hide behind. Anyone who has a brain and wants to try a hold-up waits in the hills up there,' Melrose said lifting his chin toward the chocolate-colored hills beyond Borrego. 'Anything to eat?'

'Lucia should have something up by now. You've just time enough to rinse off at the pump,' Black said as Archie led the sweating team away toward the corral.

'Old Archie,' Kyle said, removing his hat to mop at his perspiring brow, 'he's cantankerous, but hc's the best hostler on the line.'

'Yes, he is,' Black said, his voice fading as one by one the passengers emerged from the stagecoach to make their way toward the station. Through long habit he studied each of the four of them. A portly little man in a bowler hat – marked him as a salesman or travelling businessman. A lanky older-looking man in black wearing a battered Stetson. Maybe a ranch owner on his way to visit relatives or escaping the summer heat for a while.

After them a passenger whom he did not study out of habit, but out of interest. A pretty little blonde girl in dark green with her small green hat set at a saucy angle, wide blue eyes looking around the station as if with surprise.

After her came a dark-eyed, clean-shaven man with a tight expression, clenching a red travelling-bag. He made no attempt to assist the young woman but seemed to be urging her to hurry up as if he had somewhere important to go.

'Shall we go in?' Kyle Melrose asked. He had returned from the pump after rinsing up and was combing his damp hair back with his fingers. 'Or don't you get hungry around here, Mr Black?' The shotgun rider trailed after him and Black glanced that way. 'His name's McCoy,' Kyle said looking at the man with the sad eyes, shotgun clenched firmly in his hand. 'I'd introduce you, but I don't

17

think he'll be long on the job.'

'Soft?' Black inquired as they made their way toward the station.

'Not exactly, but just sort of unsuited, you might say.'

'Not many are suited for his job,' Cameron Black said.

'How about you, Black? Are you suited to this job you have?'

'I'm still here,' was all Cameron said in response.

Whitey, who was nowhere to be found when Cameron needed him to fill the water troughs, appeared out of nowhere as the smell of Lucia's fresh cornbread and coffee came to meet them. Well, he would talk to Whitey later, although it usually did as much good as talking to a stump. The kid lived in his own small world which was structured around repetition. He had been sent to cut wood, and he would cut wood until the sun went down, but he would not be diverted from one task to take on another.

Cameron escorted Kyle into the dining room, which remained relatively cool thanks to the thick adobe walls. The travelers were enjoying their breakfast which, Cameron noticed in passing, was cornbread and thick slices of meat cut off the last of the four hams in the smokehouse. There were no eggs. Coyotes, and at least once a bobcat, had gotten into the chicken house, destroying it and the birds. Their provisions were getting low. Cameron would have to start demanding that the people in Santa Fe honor their obligations – if they wanted hungry stage passengers fed at all. He determined to add a little note to the end of Virginia's request. Maybe it would do no good, but it would make him feel better.

Along the plank table, lingering over coffee, Cameron saw Kyle Melrose and McCoy, his shotgun rider, in close conversation, probably concerned about the possibility of bandits when they began their ascent into the Chocolate Mountains. Further along the table he saw the man he had taken for a salesman and the cowboy, unspeaking, and the nervous-looking citizen with the wary eyes seated by himself. He did not see the young blonde, and figured that Virginia had guided her to a place where the woman could clean up.

Lucia appeared briefly in the doorway to the kitchen, perspiration beading her brow, a lank dark curl dangling across her forehead.

'Everything all right?' Cameron asked.

'No one complained,' Lucia said with a weak smile. 'Now all I have to do is wash the dishes and

19

start on the meal for the eastbound stage.'

'I'm going to try to find someone to help you out, Lucia, but people looking for work don't come by every day – maybe an ad could be placed in the Santa Fe newspapers.'

'Who would want to take a job in this hell!' Lucia asked, and she re-entered her furnace-like kitchen. A moment later pots and pans were being hurled around again. Although they needed Lucia, Cameron found himself wishing that the lost Renaldo would return before the young woman went insane.

Philip Kramer – for that was the name of the clean-shaven man with the tight expression – got up from the table before the others and made his way out into the yard, still carrying his red carpet-bag. He crossed the yard and made his way toward the woodpile where Whitey had been working. Kramer slipped behind the pile of stacked wood and stuffed the bag into a gap between the lowest logs. Standing back, he wiped his forehead, looked around for observing eyes and then studied his hiding-place.

It would have to do. Kramer could not risk carrying the bag any further. Hiding it was like a weight being lifted from him. Although hiding it was risky, it was more risky to continue west with it.

If the stage stopped, as it usually did when it crossed paths with the eastbound coach, he could tell Tinker where the bag was hidden – if the gunfighter had not missed his connections and had failed to catch the eastbound as scheduled. For Kramer's part, he could not care – he had done his bit in this wretched affair. Now it was up to the professionals.

Upon returning to the station he saw that Archie Tate had already finished hitching the new team to the coach. A stupid-looking blond-haired kid was holding the harness to keep the team from wandering. Now the others began streaming from the adobe way station and Kramer clambered aboard, feeling relieved but still a little nervous. If something went wrong. . . .

The manager of the way station, a tall man with curly dark hair stood on the porch with his wife – a woman who must have been fine-looking in her day and was still attractive in her middle years. Why did the station-manager look familiar? Philip Kramer shook his head. If they had ever met it had been years ago and was of no importance just then. The salesman, Edward Pope was his name, climbed aboard followed by the Texan, who was so taciturn that they had never gotten his name.

Kyle Melrose was up in the box now, Van McCoy

following after. Melrose took the reins to the four-horse team and shouted out: 'Everyone aboard?' slapped the flanks of the horses with the leather straps and started them out of Borrego.

Virginia and Cameron stood beneath the porch awning, watching the coach pull out, grow smaller on the desert and eventually disappear from vision. How many stagecoaches had they watched departing for far away places, and how many more would they stand and watch? It seemed like a thin and unsatisfying life at times, but then they reflected on what life had been before Borrego and they were thankful. Tonight the sun would tilt over behind the mountains, sundown would come with a flourish and color the sky, the desert would cool and they would find themselves together in their bed, safe and content.

You really don't need much more in this life.

'Señor Black,' Lucia said from the doorway where she stood fanning the heat from her face. 'What am I supposed to do with the blonde woman?'

TWO

'She's in my kitchen,' Lucia explained. 'I thought nothing of it – many women are interested in seeing other people's kitchens. Then, as the coach was being prepared to depart, she seemed to huddle in the corner near the pantry as if she were a small, frightened animal. I realized she did not want to travel on. What was I to say? It's not my business. But I don't know what to do with her.'

'We'll handle it,' Virginia said, looking at Cameron.

'Why don't you handle it,' Cameron said.

'Woman's work, is it?'

'Most likely, don't you think?'

'The longer I know you, the more I believe you are intimidated by women!' Virginia said.

'Why wouldn't I be – with my experiences?'

23

Cameron said. Virginia did not know how to take that remark. Probably it was a wobbly joke. 'Besides, I've got to try to find a deer before the day's over, or we'll all end up eating sand.'

'I was thinking,' Virginia said as they started into the adobe, 'what if we could capture a covey of quail? Then we'd have them and even quail eggs!'

'That's a fine idea,' Cameron answered drily. 'I'll leave that task to you, since it's your idea. For myself, I'm better at bringing down a deer than chasing a bunch of birds around the desert.'

'Because it involves using a gun,' Virginia said, her temper rising a little. She did not like being mocked.

'Yes, dear. Because of that.' He kissed her nose and walked away toward the gun rack to retrieve his Winchester. 'Meanwhile, you'd better find out why the blonde missed her stage.'

'You have all the fun, Cam.'

'Want to trade? I could do without lying on hot rocks all afternoon, waiting for a clean shot at a deer, gutting it, and carrying it back.'

'Oh, do what you want!' Virginia said, still half-angry. 'I suppose you're right: we both should stick to what we're best at.'

Cameron gave her a small, gratified smile, took his rifle and started out toward Bent Creek – the

24

most likely place to find a deer.

Virginia turned and followed an uncertain Lucia into the heated kitchen. The girl was there, sitting on a low stool in the corner of the room near the larder, her hands clasped together between her knees. She looked up at Virginia with haunted eyes. She had lost her green hat somewhere and her hair hung loose across her shoulders. She was very young, between eighteen and twenty, Virginia guessed, and quite shaken.

'Well?' Virginia demanded. The girl's lips quivered. Her blue eyes searched Virginia's.

'What do you mean?' the blonde asked.

'I think you know what I mean,' Virginia replied. 'Who are you, and more important, what are you doing here?'

'I'm Becky Grant,' the girl said rising from the stool, 'and I'm here because I have no place else to go.'

Lucia was in and out of the room, bringing in plates and utensils from the dining area. The iron stove continued to give off an enormous amount of heat.

'Let's go outside,' Virginia suggested in a softer voice. It was hardly cool outside. A warm breeze ruffled the leaves of the cottonwood trees, doing little to alleviate the wicked heat of the sun. The two women sat on a bench in the shade of the trees. Virginia faced Becky and asked her:

'What do you mean, you have no place to go? Obviously you were headed somewhere when you boarded the stage back in Santa Fe.'

'I didn't want to go – there,' Becky answered in a muffled voice that threatened to become tearful.

Virginia didn't want to pry. The girl obviously had some personal problems. She tried gently to nudge Becky. 'Look, you can stay here until the next westbound comes through – maybe that will give you enough time to consider what you're doing, but you can't expect us to—'

'I can work!' Becky said anxiously. 'Maybe you don't think so because I'm in my Sunday best, but I'm a country girl and I'm used to hard work. I can help your cook in there – I'll do dishes, scrub pots. Anything! But I can't travel on.'

'I'd have to talk to my husband,' Virginia said. The girl's eyes were wide with fear, nearly panic-stricken. Whatever, whoever she was afraid of had her on the verge of breaking down. 'Do you have other clothes with you?' Virginia asked, rising.

'I . . . just let my luggage go along with the stage,' Becky said. 'I can work in this,' she said, rubbing her hands down across her green velvet dress.

'No you can't,' Virginia said. 'I'll look around and see what I can find for you to wear.'

Cameron was out for nearly three hours, slipping around and among the rocks lining the banks of Bent Creek. There was no water running in the sandy river-bottom, not at this time of year, but there was still some standing water in a few catch basins. These were where the deer and other desert animals came to drink. The trouble was that it was close to high noon, the sun was glaring down and the usual watering times for the animals were just after dawn and again at dusk.

The rocks which Cameron Black scrambled among were as heated as irons. He worked his way down to a slot between the rocks and found a patch of clear ground to lie on and watch a catch basin, which was shaded by a row of nearly black, summer-struck willows crowding the dry river's bank. He was not enjoying the day, but the provisions at the way station were low and all he was getting from Santa Fe were promises – easy to chew on, but hardly nourishing.

His patience paid off at last. Approaching cautiously from the willows a four-point mule deer arrived at the pond, dipping its head to drink. For just a moment Cameron regretted having to take the animal down, but there would be hungry people traveling through, and with the beef low, the ham gone, a venison steak or two would hold them until steers could be brought through from Santa Fe.

Cameron fixed the front bead sight on the animal, aiming just behind the shoulder and triggered off. Only one bullet was necessary; it was a heart shot. The rifle's report had scattered a flock of roosting crows in the willows and they took to wing in a raucous black cloud. Cameron made his way down the slope, slipping and sliding over the rocks and loose soil, and recovered his deer.

It was a big old buck, but Lucia was a wonder with tenderizing stringy meat with her secret marinade. Cameron placed his rifle aside, hung the deer by its rack in a willow tree and began field-dressing it, drawing a swarm of interested flies to smother his face in the heat of the day. After that all there was to do was shoulder the deer, carry it up out of the rocky canyon and take it home, where he would skin it out and butcher it.

Sometimes he missed town life.

On arriving at the way station he let the buck drop from his weary shoulders. He was bruised and heat-exhausted. Age was making inroads, he decided. When he was a kid . . . but he was no longer a kid and hadn't been for a long while. He had let his life flow by in an uninterrupted, violent stream of living only for the moment. Virginia appeared on the back porch.

'Home is the hunter,' she said drolly.

'Yes, and I wish you had traded jobs with me, Ginnie.' He seated himself on the rough hewn bench on the rear porch. Inside the house he heard the two young women laughing as they worked in the kitchen.

'What. . . ?'

'I let her stay – Becky – the young blonde.'

'Sounds like she's having a good time,' Cameron said. It was the first time in memory that he had heard any sounds of merriment in the kitchen. Normally by now Lucia would have resumed her pot-throwing and complaining.

'Maybe misery really does love company,' Virginia said.

'How long's the girl going to stay?'

'We haven't discussed that. I was waiting for you, Cam.'

'Can we afford to keep her around? You're the bookkeeper.'

'For a little while anyway. The girl's frightened out of her mind about something, Cameron. I haven't been able to find out what, yet.'

29

'Oh, well,' he said rising, 'so long as Lucia is a little happier. I was getting afraid to put my head in her kitchen, waiting for the next pot to hit my skull.'

'What are you going to do now?' Virginia asked. 'The eastbound stage is due in an hour or so.'

'I'm going to find my skinning knife and a whetstone,' Cameron answered, nodding at the carcass of the deer. 'Unless you want to change jobs with me.'

'We should both stick to what we're best at,' Virginia said with a smile. 'I'm going to supervise the girls for a while and then get back to the books, check the list of supplies. It really does have to get off to Santa Fe today.'

'While I have all the fun.'

'While you have all the fun, dear,' Virginia said, kissing him.

'I could use some help. Where's Whitey?'

'You sent him out this morning to chop wood, didn't you?'

'Yes.'

'Well?' Virginia asked. They both knew the boy, once started, would chop wood until there was no more to be found.

Virginia's smile fell away suddenly. 'We have company,' she said, her eyes fixed on the shadowed figure moving through the stand of cotton-wood trees. Cameron Black turned that way as well. His hand instinctively went to his hip where he no longer wore a gun these days. Even at this distance they could see the slanting sun glinting on the silver badge the man was wearing on his leather vest.

'Cam. . . .' Virginia said nervously, touching his arm.

'He doesn't want me,' Cameron said. 'There are no warrants out on me.'

'You can't be sure of that, can you?'

'No.'

Because there were too many backtrails, too many ill-advised shooting scrapes. In half a hundred towns across most of the Southwest. No, he could not be certain that somewhere he was not still wanted by the law: the price a man paid for a lifetime of carrying guns for hire.

'Maybe it's the girl!' Virginia said, gripping his arm tightly. 'She's afraid of something.'

'Better put her someplace until we can figure this out,' Cameron said, and in the meantime he had picked up his deer rifle again.

Virginia entered the house, not rushing. She had seen much in her time, and knew better than to arouse the lawman's curiosity by hurrying. As

31

the rider on the buckskin horse drew nearer, Cameron could make out the badge of a county sheriff. The man was steely-eyed, bulky through the shoulders, dressed in a white shirt with a leather vest over it, faded black jeans and a wide-brimmed, once-white Stetson. He approached the house and gave Cameron a two-finger salute, touching the brim of his hat.

'Mind if I step down? I've had a long ride.'

'Come ahead,' Cameron said, now placing his rifle aside again. He had no wish to appear belligerent.

'My name's Link Beaton, out of Alamogordo.'

'You're a long way from home,' Cameron commented.

'I am,' Sheriff Beaton said with what might have been meant as a smile. 'Have you got water for my pony?'

'I'll show you the way,' Cam offered. Then casually he asked, 'Is there trouble up this way?'

'Just a matter of a missing fifty-thousand dollars,' Beaton said as they walked his horse toward the corral.

'Fifty. . . .' Cameron was truly amazed.

'I tracked the thief – or one of them – to Santa Fe and was told that he had taken the stage west.'

'I see,' Cameron said, trying not to show his

relief. His own past, then, had nothing to do with the sheriff's visit, nor did the problems of Becky. Unless. . . .

'What did this man look like?' Cameron inquired as they took the buckskin horse into the corral to drink at the trough with a few of the station horses while Sheriff Beaton loosened the animal's cinches, preparing to unsaddle.

'I don't have a real good description of him,' Beaton said, swinging his saddle from the horse's back.

Again Cameron was relieved – it was a man Beaton was looking for then, and not a young blonde woman. Archie Tate came wandering out of the barn to meet them, and Cameron asked, 'Archie, will you see that the sheriff's horse is cooled down properly and then grained? It's had a long ride.' The always taciturn Archie only nodded, stroked his beard and shrewdly calculated how much water the weary horse should be allowed to drink at this time.

Cameron said, 'Your horse is in good hands, Sheriff. Can we offer you our hospitality? There should be coffee on, and dinner is being prepared for the eastbound stage passengers.'

From the front porch of the station Virginia was watching, her dark eyes unreadable to anyone but

33

Cameron, who read concern lingering there. As they reached the doorway, Sheriff Beaton touched his hat brim to Virginia. He had begun studying Cameron on their stroll back as well. Twice he seemed about to say something, but had not.

'You might ask our cooks if they have anything up for the sheriff to eat,' Cameron said. He had slightly emphasized the plural to let Virginia know that Beaton was not looking for Becky and it was safe for her to come out. 'I've got to get to that deer before it starts to dry out'

'Of course,' Beaton, who had noticed the deer, nodded. But before Cameron Black could turn away, he asked, 'Don't I know you from somewhere?'

'I can't imagine where,' Cameron said. The sheriff answered with a further nod, but continued to let his puzzled eyes linger on Cameron.

'One of the girls will show you where to wash up,' Virginia said, steering the marshal into the station. She let him make his own way and returned to Cameron. 'Do you think he does?' she asked anxiously.

'Does what?'

'Know you from somewhere.'

Cameron shook his head heavily. 'I don't know, Ginnie. I really don't. I have been so many places.'

34

'Well then, what does he want way out here?' she asked, and briefly Cameron told her what the sheriff had told him.

'Now,' he said, 'if you will excuse me – I really had better take care of that deer. We can't afford to be wasting meat.'

The gunman's name was Renaldo del Campo. He had not meant to become a gunman, but he had. Leaving his poor village, he had taken a vow to go out into the world and make his fortune. Fortunes were hard to come by out on the desert. With his black silk scarf over his face no one could have recognized him, even had he been a known figure. With his three companions, he waited in the scattered pines along the trail leading into the highlands of the Chocolate Mountains as the stagecoach from the east labored up the switchback trail along the flank of the hills.

'What do you think it's carrying?' one of his companions, a stocky man called Fuego asked.

'No telling. But more than we've got in our pockets, that's for sure,' Renaldo answered.

'Gold, I know it's gold,' another of their band, Carlos, said, his eyes glittering. Carlos was the most excitable of their band of robbers. He envisioned a fortune to be made before each robbery, and was

35

disappointed when nothing more than pocket change was found in the stores, trading posts, mining camps and occasional stagecoaches that they stuck up. His optimism was not infectious, but each of them believed that sooner or later they would run across a large score, if only on account of the numbers of robberies they pulled off.

They were famous – infamous – already, from Sonora to Phoenix and points north. There was a heavy bounty out on them, worth more than the amount they had stolen. But they had caused enough trouble to become an irritation. And there were four men behind them who would not be dead if it were not for Renaldo's gang.

That was mostly Sabato's doing. The little man was too quick to open fire when he was disappointed.

As the stagecoach continued its slow rumbling way toward them, the four men took up their positions behind the rocks through which the coach must pass and waited in the heat of day. Renaldo was thinking – let this be a rich one. He had left his pueblo to become wealthy. But as of now he was only ten dollars wealthier than he had been then. He had lost more than he had gained. His home, his way of life, his Lucia.

Standing now beside Fuego, he could feel the

perspiration trickling down his side; it seemed that it was less from the heat than from fear, but fear must be controlled or a man is nothing. For the third time he quickly rechecked the loads in his pistol. The stage was so near now that he could hear the clopping of the horse's hoofs, the complaint of an ungreased wheel.

'Is there a shotgun?' the stubby little Fuego asked, himself appearing nervous. This was only his second hold-up.

'There's always a shotgun,' Renaldo said. 'And don't forget there will be guns inside the stage.'

'I won't forget.'

Renaldo looked across the trail to where Carlos and Sabato, similarly concealed, waited. Renaldo risked one quick look down the trail. When he judged the moment to be right he nodded and stepped out into the path of the stagecoach, his pistol held high. It was a gamble, attacking it in broad daylight. But Renaldo had weighed his chances of success against the humiliation of returning to Lucia, to his home, against that and felt it was a risk he had to take. There weren't going to be many opportunities like this one.

Kyle Melrose, who had been half-dozing as he guided the team of horses across the desert road, came suddenly alert. A man wearing a white shirt and black trousers stood in the middle of the road, pistol trained on him. He nudged his shotgun rider, Van McCoy with his elbow, but McCoy had already seen the bandit, and as a second man, a stocky, swarthy man emerged from the rocks, McCoy cut loose with both barrels of his ten-gauge express gun. The taller man dove for the cover of the rocks, firing his pistol twice as he went. The stubby little man remained where he was, on his face in the dust.

Now from the other side of the road two more men appeared. One of them fired twice from his knee, and the second shot took Van McCoy in the chest. McCoy pitched forward out of the box and fell to the earth as the horses reared up in panic. From inside the coach three men boiled out to join in the fight. The tall Texan gunned one of the remaining bandits down with a head shot. The man beside him – Philip Kramer – had the bad luck to be shot in the heart as he stepped down from the coach.

The small man with the derby hat – the businessman – met with the same fate. His response had been to emerge from the stagecoach and hold his hands high in surrender, but the remaining highwayman cut him down all the same. Kyle

Melrose was still fighting to restrain his panicked team when he saw the tall Texan level his pistol again and quite calmly gun down the remaining robber. This one pirouetted, clutched his chest, threw his gun away and danced his way into his grave.

One of the robbers, the one with the black silk scarf across his face had gotten away, but Kyle Melrose was not paid to chase down bandits. The quiet Texan climbed up onto the seat beside Kyle and said:

'It's just the two of us left, partner. We'd better be moving on.'

Kyle agreed, and as quickly as possible he drove the stage through the rocky pass, still handling the nervous horses cautiously. After the pass was cleared Kyle flicked the horses' ears with his whip and sent them into a wild run across the flats. He hated to misuse the animals that way, but he hated the idea of joining the dead even more.

Renaldo watched the coach fly past him. He walked out to study the dead men, biting back a curse. His arm hurt – he had taken a few pellets of buckshot from the shotgun blast. Now what? The sun was merciless, the land empty, his prospects bleak. He sat on a low rock and tipped his hat back. He was not even a good criminal.

What now!

As the flies buzzed around him, gathering in the wake of the dead, Renaldo made his decision. There was nothing for him but to return home in disgrace. He brightened slightly at the thought of Lucia's welcoming arms as he returned to Borrego to tell her that he was finished with his long-riding days. Having her with him might be enough to assuage the shame of failure. He would marry her, embrace her comfort and find some menial job in the pueblo. It was that or . . . he studied the earth littered with dead bodies.

He was finished with his life of crime.

Weary but distantly optimistic, Renaldo returned to where he had picketed his gray horse, swung heavily into the saddle and pointed the horse's nose toward Borrego Springs.

THREE

As the coach rolled into Overton, trailing dust into the heated sky, Perry Tinker emerged from the bordello and made his way to the depot, moving with a confident swagger as he finished tucking his shirt-tails in. This was it then – $50,000 lifted from the branch bank in Alamogordo were on the coach.

He grew suddenly uneasy. There were only two men aboard the stage: the driver and a man dressed in black who definitely was not Philip Kramer. Where was their courier, then? He stepped toward the stage station a little more quickly, settling the Colt revolver he carried on his hip. He had invested a lot of time and taken a huge risk in obtaining the money. Somehow he had let Frank Belavia talk him into letting Kramer

41

– Belavia's half-brother – transport the $50,000 for them, explaining that if they were tracked down and discovered to have none of the bank funds on them, it would be a hard case to prove against them.

But where was Kramer!

Tinker continued on now at a measured pace toward the stage depot where several men were engaged in a conversation consisting of complaints and sharp questions. He heard one man, who appeared to be the local law asking: 'How many did they get?'

'Everyone except for me and this man,' Kyle Melrose said, nodding at the tall Texan. 'There were four of them; they jumped us at Eagle Pass.'

'Can you identify any of them?' the lawman asked.

'I didn't stop to look at the bodies,' Melrose answered stiffly. 'There was still one man standing and we had little time for that.'

'Could you describe that one?' the lawman persisted.

'Behind a mask? No, fairly tall, probably Spanish – that's all I can tell you.' Melrose dabbed at his face with a bandanna. 'If you want to go out there and identify them, they're still lying on the ground, thanks to poor Van McCoy and our friend here,' he placed a hand briefly on the Texan's shoulder.

'And your name, sir?'

'Ben McCulloch, formerly a Texas Ranger. Now retired and pleased with it.'

'All right, then,' the local lawman said. He was short, stout and apparently out of his depth. 'We'll send some of the deputies out to try to identify the robbers. Was anything taken?'

'Nothing,' Melrose answered, 'but then we weren't carrying anything worth the taking in the first place. Either the gang had some bad information or it was a crime of opportunity.'

It was neither, Perry Tinker knew as he listened in on the conversation. Someone had managed to discover that Kramer had the $50,000 with him, and had set their sights on that particular coach. Now Kramer was dead and the money from the Alamogordo job was missing!

The question was, where was it?

Tinker watched as the baggage was removed from the boot of the stagecoach, looking for anything that might resemble Kramer's carpetbag, then he walked slowly back to the hotel where he meant to malign and curse Frank Belavia for causing this. The loss of $50,000 can rekindle a lot of forgotten curses. Tinker, who had not at first objected to Belavia's plan, admitting that it wouldn't do to get caught red-handed with the stolen money, now felt that he had been played for a fool, the money not having arrived in Overton. He doubted that Philip Kramer had the nerve to try double-crossing him; the little man flinched every time he saw a gun.

He hated to suspect Frank's half-brother, but while Tinker was wandering around with no more than a few silver coins in his pocket, Frank Belavia seemed unconcerned – he must have some capital from someplace else. Believing that Belavia would not rob him, either, that left him few other suspects. The rest of the band of robbers – Duane Pembroke and Satchel Rose – had been with Tinker the entire time. That only left one man: Renaldo del Campo.

Tinker brooded over this at the saloon. Renaldo knew their plans, but he had told them that, along with some old friends, he was going to attempt another job, and was then going to find his woman in Borrego, and bring her to Overton in time for the split of the bank money.

It had to be Renaldo who had crossed them. He matched the stage driver's vague description. He had the entire $50,000, and was probably now riding for the border. He might make it, too,

Tinker thought, but he wouldn't live long enough to spend all that money.

Tinker slapped his empty whiskey glass down on the bar and walked off to find Pembroke and Rose. They had some riding to do.

Whitey was still chopping wood as the sky began to grow dark. Cameron Black went to the thin blond kid and placed a hand on his shoulder.

'That's enough, Whitey, come in and eat.'

Shirtless, Whitey, looked up from his work, indicating with his hands that there was still wood remaining to be split.

'It will keep until tomorrow,' Cameron said. 'Besides, the eastbound coach is due and Archie might need your help.'

And the eastbound coach was indeed due: Cameron knew this not from a clock, but because Archie Tate had emerged from one of his hiding-places, scratching at his head, tugging at his beard, moving toward the corral. What sort of sixth sense Archie had, he did not know, but in less than five minutes, a coach could be heard in the distance rumbling toward the station, sending dust clouds into the sunset sky.

Dinner was supposed to be venison, Indian pota-toes, corn bread and beans according to Lucia, and that sounded fine to Cameron Black just then. He wandered toward the station, passing the four penned cattle who watched him stupidly, not knowing that they were doomed. They seemed to be low on fodder; Cameron would have to remind Whitey later to fork some hay for them. The cattle must survive if they were going to survive themselves out on the long desert.

Lucia lifted her head. A horse was approaching the back yard and her heart leaped. It could not be! But she clung to her eternal hope and when she swung the back door of the kitchen wide, this time it *was* Renaldo! She left Becky Grant to the stirring of the pots, the frying of the venison steaks, and rushed out into the still, purple silence of the evening.

'Renaldo!' she breathed, finding it hard to believe that her long-riding man had actually returned, and though she had imagined this moment hundreds of times she did not know how to manage it.

Renaldo swung down from his gray horse's back and stretched out his arms. Lucia rushed into his embrace, saying a dozen foolish, muted things against his chest.

'Is it over, Renaldo?' she asked as he held her at

arm's length, 'Can we go home and start a family, grow old together?'

'I think it is over,' Renaldo del Campo said. 'But I'm not sure. There is trouble behind me.'

'What have you done?' Lucia asked, not shocked, but deeply concerned.

'Some things I am not proud of,' Renaldo admitted.

'Is the law looking for you?'

'I don't know,' he answered.

Lucia flinched beneath his grip. 'Renaldo! There is a sheriff from Alamogordo here. Is he looking for you?'

'I don't know,' was all that Renaldo could say. His eyes shifted suspiciously toward the back of the adobe way station.

'You cannot come in,' Lucia said nervously. 'I will bring you a plate of food.'

'I won't leave without you,' Renaldo said with a certainty he had never voiced before.

'No – I won't let you,' Lucia said, her fingers toying with the sleeves of his white shirt. 'Let me think for a minute, I will ask Señor Black or the *señora* if you can stay here for the night – in the barn, maybe. I will tell them you are my brother. They will not refuse; I am certain of that.'

'If you think so,' Renaldo said wearily. He had

47

ridden long that day; his wounded shoulder ached. There was no way they could ride away on that evening with no particular goal decided upon. If things had gone differently – he had pictured it in his mind, riding in with his share of $50,000 and sweeping Lucia up in his arms. Ah, well, things do not go as well as they are imagined. But he had his Lucia again, and that was a beginning.

'In the meantime, keep out of the sight of this sheriff,' Lucia insisted. Renaldo had already figured on doing that, if he could. Could he be connected with the Alamogordo bank robbery? He had no idea. If Tinker had not gunned down two men in the streets while they were making their escape, if Kramer had delivered the money to them . . . life is a sequence of 'ifs', it seemed.

In front of Renaldo, hovering, was the law. Behind him, he knew, was the notorious gunman Perry Tinker. In fact Renaldo had not known that the gang's money was supposed to be aboard the stagecoach. Someone had let something slip in Alamogordo about there being a large amount of cash on the westbound stage. Belavia and Tinker had both said that they thought it was time to cool their heels for a while. Renaldo was anxious to get his own plan going and didn't want to miss this opportunity, so he had bid goodbye to the robbers and, ill-advisedly, collected his old friends Fuego, Carlos and Sabato to help him halt the stage, hoping to have twice the money he was planning on to start a new life with Lucia.

Now he had none. He had been figuring on making his way to Overton, with Lucia at his side, and collecting his share of the bank robbery's profit.

But for this evening, he was content, eating his dinner cooked by Lucia's own hands, as he sat on the bench under the trees behind the way station. That could be enough of a life to make it worth living, he thought. An outlaw's life was for fools. Go back home, dine on beans and tortillas, watch babies crawling around the floor, listen to Lucia humming softly in the kitchen. She had never wanted him to hit the long trail; in fact she would be ashamed of him if he admitted what he had been doing, though surely she must have some sort of an idea of what he had been up to.

Renaldo looked up at the sound of soft approaching footsteps to see Lucia, pretty and appealing in the moonlight as she walked toward him, her long dark hair falling like silk across her shoulders.

'Is that lawman still here?' he asked in a low voice after she had settled beside him on the

49

bench and given him a soft kiss.

'Yes,' she whispered. 'I think he's going to stay for a while, though I don't know why. He didn't tell anybody. I talked to the *señora*. I told her you were a cousin to me, and she has agreed to let you sleep in the barn. I don't think they believed me, but I do my work here and they will do me this small favor.'

'You didn't mention my name?'

'No. What would be the point in that?' She had taken his hand between her own two small ones.

Her eyes were luminous in the moonlight. Renaldo told her, 'Lucia, I think we should be traveling on in the morning.'

'Because of the sheriff?'

'He's one reason.' Renaldo hesitated. 'I still have some unfinished business in Overton. When that is completed we can return home, to the pueblo and find our happiness.'

'I do not like leaving that quickly,' she said, looking down and away. 'The Blacks have been good to me, and they need to have a cook here.'

'What about that other girl? I saw her moving behind the window.'

'Becky? She is a nice girl, Renaldo. But she is only a child, really. She doesn't know what to do in the kitchen. Besides . . . I think she is running away from something and will not stay here long.'

'Running away . . .' Renaldo repeated. *Like us?* And that was what he was inviting Lucia to share with him – a lifetime of hiding out, avoiding the law wherever they went. Briefly his heart sank and he deeply regretted ever having taken part in the business of crime. Already Carlos, Sabato and Fuego were dead, along with those two men Tinker had killed outside the bank and the three unknown men on the stagecoach.

And it had profited him nothing. Originally he thought that just having money would bring him peace of mind. How stupid could he have been! Even if he managed to get his share of the money from Belavia and Tinker it would provide him and Lucia small comfort if the law found him and strung him up for murder. That would be a nice way for their love to end!

There were no more romantic outlaws. They were historical fantasies.

Lucia took his empty tray as they rose, Renaldo saying, 'I'd better slip away toward the barn. The sheriff is not sleeping there, is he?'

'No – they have given him a bed in the station. Renaldo . . .' she began anxiously, but found herself unable to finish her thought. Something was wrong here, and she did not know what it was.

'I have a lot of work to do now; the stage is arriving. Get some sleep, Renaldo – we will talk in the morning.'

Halting in the moon-shadows beside the way station, Renaldo peered out. The eastbound stagecoach had braked to a halt. A man with a strong face and dark hair stood on the porch with a woman in dark blue beside him. These, he took it, were the Blacks. A slender older woman was helped from the stage, and a big-shouldered man with close-cropped hair stepped down, looking around him with disgust. The driver of the coach and the shotgun rider swung down with practiced ease.

'What do you say, Mr Black!' the driver, a narrow and sun-swarthy man named Jennings, asked as Archie Tate appeared from nowhere, as always, and led the used team away.

'Not much news here,' Cameron Black answered. 'What about you?'

'They held up Kyle Melrose's stage. Killed Van McCoy and two passengers.'

'Good lord!' Virginia Black said.

'Yup,' the driver said. 'You can bet me and Harvey,' he nodded at the shotgun rider, 'didn't slow down for a second when we hit Eagle Pass.'

'That's where it happened, then?'

'That's where. Let's step inside if we may – let me wrap myself around a cup of coffee and I'll tell you about it. All that I know, that is.'

Renaldo remained in the shadows for a while longer, even though he knew that no one there could possibly connect him with the coach hold-up. The moon was riding high and the breeze strengthening as Renaldo crossed the clearing between house and barn and started in. Just as he was entering the building, he happened to glance back and see someone watching him. The moon-light gleamed off Sheriff Link Beaton's silver badge.

'Did everyone have enough to eat?' Lucia asked. Her face looked drawn with some private sorrow as she cleared away the dishes from the plank tables. Everyone nodded or murmured thanks. Becky had remained in the kitchen during the meal; now she emerged to assist in collecting the dishes. As Cameron watched her, her eyes widened. She gawked. The blond man with the closely shorn hair and lantern jaw rose from his seat, pointed and said:

'So here you are,' he said. Becky Grant seemed frozen with fear, like some small rabbit. Cameron rose from his chair, not liking this. The big man said to the trembling girl, 'I ought to wring your neck.'

'You're not going to do any such thing,' Cameron Black said, planting himself in front of the blond man.

'You don't know a thing about this, mister. I'd be obliged if you'd just step out of my way.' The small commotion had now caught the attention of Link Beaton who had just returned from outside.

'I don't need to know anything,' Cameron Black said. 'This is my station, my home – you might say my own little kingdom. And Becky is working for me.' The blond man was half a head taller that Cam, and now he glared at him with menacing eyes. His hand rested on his holstered pistol.

'Get out of my way,' the big man snarled.

'Don't start anything you can't finish,' Sheriff Beaton said from the doorway, and the big man spun that way in a fury before noticing the star on Beaton's vest.

'I'd advise you to sit down,' Beaton said with the competent coolness of an experienced lawman.

'That girl. . . .' the tall man sputtered, pointing toward Becky who had already ducked into the kitchen.

'Is she your wife? A relative? Has she committed a crime?' Beaton asked in a reasonable tone.

'No, but—'

'I'd advise you again to sit down,' Beaton told him. 'I'd hate to have gunsmoke for dessert after a good meal.'

'What do you think that was about?' Virginia asked as she and Cameron relaxed in their room.

'I don't know. Can't you ask Becky?'

'She'd be more likely to tell Lucia,' Virginia said, brushing her hair. 'Becky seems to look upon me as a sort of mother figure.' Virginia frowned at her own face in the mirror and placed the brush aside.

'You could be, you know,' Cameron Black said from his position on the bed where he lay on his back, clasped hands behind his head.

'Be what?'

'A mother figure if you had a child.' Cam responded.

'I don't see what . . . oh, no! What are you suggesting?'

'I think you know. I am a man.'

'I've noticed that,' Virginia said, sitting on the bed beside him. Her smile was sweetly sad, then, whatever her reply was going to be, she abruptly changed subjects.

'Speaking of Lucia,' she said as Cameron's hand

crept up her arm.

'I wasn't.'

'Speaking of Lucia,' Virginia went on, 'who do you think this so-called cousin of hers really is?'

'I think he's the longed-for Renaldo, don't you? I haven't heard a pan thrown in the kitchen all evening.'

'I think you're right,' Virginia said as Cameron Black's hand continued its creeping, 'but why try to hoodwink us?'

'I can think of half a hundred reasons,' Cameron said, 'but I don't want to just now.' He drew her face down to his and kissed her deeply.

'When everyone's gone,' Virginia said, gently pushing him away.

Outside a faint susurrating sound had turned into a shrilling whistle. Cameron reluctantly sat up in bed as the wind began to moan and complain around the adobe way station. The cottonwood trees were rattling branch against branch outside.

'Just my luck,' Cameron said, rising to stamp into his boots. 'No one is going anywhere for a while. We've got a sandstorm brewing. Better get dressed again and see if we can plug up all the chinks in this old place.'

Cameron found Archie Tate sitting in the

dining room, drinking coffee. Somehow it didn't surprise him. The man had an uncanny sense of what was going on around him. Archie should have been out harnessing the horses for the next leg of the coach's trip, but some instinct had warned him that there was a dust storm coming. Horses that cannot breathe in such a storm or find their way in the darkness were doomed.

'I saw the moon go orange and begin to fade,' Archie said by way of explanation. 'I figured I might as well give it up as a bad job.'

'You were right,' said Cameron. 'Want to give me a hand stuffing towels under the doors and around the windows?'

Virginia was already busy trying to figure out where everyone could sleep. The older woman who had gotten off the stagecoach, one Mrs Birch, started complaining in a shrill voice that she could not afford to miss this night's travel.

The stage driver patiently told her that they had no other option. The horses would suffocate or lose their way; they would not be able to see the trail. They risked disaster trying to cross the desert under these conditions.

And he was not exaggerating; the storm had come in with noise and a fury which swamped the way station with drifting sand. Outside, the dust clouds were impenetrable. The moon had disappeared behind the curtain of swirling sand. The driver had been worried about his team, of course, but Archie told them that all of the horses were safely sheltered inside the barn.

When Whitey Carroll managed to fight his way through the dust and heated blast of the wind he just stared wildly at them. His face was coated with dirt, and his clothes were dust-streaked. He walked up to Cameron and stuttered something incomprehensible before telling Cam, 'The whole place is blowing away out there!'

'Did you get the cattle into the barn?' Virginia asked Archie Tate.

'Cattle are no part of my job,' Archie answered stiffly.

And they weren't, but they were a part of Cameron Black's. 'I'll hie them over. Whitey, will you go with me?'

Whitey blinked uncomprehendingly at Cam. His words might have been spoken in a foreign tongue so far as Whitey Carroll was concerned. Today had been a wood day; why was the boss asking about cattle! Rather than take the time waiting for Whitey's thoughts to order themselves, Cameron simply turned the puzzled kid toward the door and guided him out into the ferocity of the dust storm.

Outside there was next to no visibility. Cameron tied his bandanna over mouth and nose and waded through the swirling dust. The wind was not steady, but gusting ferociously now and then, driving sand with the force of shotgun pellets against exposed flesh. Cam looked for, but could not see Whitey. Or much else.

It was his own yard, though, and Cameron waded through the lashing storm to the cattle pen with only a little confusion. He took a coil of rope from a post and opened the gate to search for the steers. Whitey caught up with him, but there was no chance of conversation above the roar and drive of the storm. Cameron made a circling motion with his hand, hoping that Whitey took his meaning. What had to be done with the con-founded cattle was to loop the rope around each set of horns, and lead them in a string toward the shelter of the barn.

Whether Whitey had seen his signal or not, he began working at doing just that. Soon they had three of the cattle so secured, but the last of them was balkier or even more confused than the others. They could not even find the reluctant steer as the veils of sand drifted past, and when Whitey did manage to locate it, the angry steer fought him off with a brief charge, lowering its horns toward the yard hand. Cursing, Cameron handed the lead rope to Whitey and started after the balky cow. He had to half-bulldog it, rodeo style, and loop the rope around the frightened animal's horns. Its sheer weight made this a dangerous stunt, but there was no choice. Pain shot up along Cameron's damaged left arm – the one that he had gotten shot in the last time he made war, but he managed to hang on and avoid the menacing horns.

In another five minutes he and Whitey had the struggling, bewildered animals lined out in the direction of the barn through the dark whirl of the sandstorm. Cameron ran ahead, ducking reflexively against the force of the storm, and swung the barn doors wide. As he did, the gunshot rang out, its report like thunder through the turmoil of the storm.

FOUR

Cameron threw himself to one side, watched a wide-eyed Whitey try to restrain the string of cattle, then darted toward the overhanging hayloft – for that was certainly where the shot had come from. Even now a wisp of powder-smoke hung in the air. Cameron Black reached the ladder leading to the loft, and began scaling it on the back side. The strain on his left arm was terrific, but it was something that had to be done. Either that or take their chances at crossing the barn across open ground to be shot down as they fled.

Clinging to the inside of the ladder, Cameron tried to locate Whitey, but the kid had taken shelter somewhere along the stalls where the stage horses were now stationed. He tried to listen for movement above him, but the force and fury of the storm made this futile. Cameron climbed several rungs higher, knowing that soon he would have no choice but to expose himself and go after the gunman above. Taking a deep breath, he switched to the front of the ladder and as quickly as possible threw himself up onto the floor of the loft, rolling behind several stacked bales of hay. No more shots were fired. Cameron tugged down his bandanna, wiped a hand back across his hair and shouted out:

'Throw out your gun and come out of there!' which seemed a foolish command seeing that Cameron was unarmed, but the ambusher could have no way of knowing that.

'Mr Black?'

'That's right,' Cameron answered, unable to recognize the voice or put a face with it.

'I have put my gun away – it's me, Lucia's cousin.'

Cameron tentatively looked over the hay bales to see a young, good-looking Spanish kid with his hands raised high.

'Damn it, Renaldo,' Cameron said angrily. 'What were you thinking?'

'I'm sorry,' the younger man stuttered. 'I thought it was someone else. I was sleeping when the doors burst open and I could not see with the sand blowing.'

Renaldo could not have been faking his dismay. Cameron walked toward him across the loft, his anger only slightly abated. He halted before Renaldo and lifted the young man's gun from his holster while Renaldo stood stock-still.

'Who did you think it was?' Cameron asked, unloading the weapon before handing it back. 'The sheriff, maybe?'

Renaldo's face showed shock. He paled and nodded. It was apparent that Beaton was exactly who he had been expecting. 'But how did you know who I am?' he asked Cameron. 'Did Lucia. . . ?'

'We guessed,' Cameron told him. 'It didn't make a lot of sense for some cousin of hers to appear suddenly off the desert, looking for her.' The younger man seemed to be ashamed. He was trembling slightly. 'You scared the hell out of my yard man, you know?' Cameron said. 'Whitey!' he called down. 'You can come out now. It's all right.'

'I am sorry,' Renaldo said miserably. 'Lucia has said that you and the Señora Black have treated her with kindness.'

'All right – it's over now,' Cameron said, his heart-rate slowing now that fear and anxiety were fading. He gestured toward two hay bales and suggested, 'Why don't we sit down and talk about this for a few minutes. I'm not a lawman; I'm not an outlaw either, but I've been in a few scrapes in my time. I just might understand. I might even be able to help you.'

They sat facing each other. The storm raged on, and although Whitey had emerged from hiding to close the barn doors, the sound of the wind-driven storm was terrific. Renaldo rubbed at his neck, shifted his feet several times, then at last began to tell Cameron what had happened, how it had happened – at least most of it. Cameron Black only listened silently, nodding from time to time. When he was finished, Renaldo said:

'Now I have quit the gang. I don't care anymore about the money. I only want my Lucia and a small place to live quietly.'

'A good decision,' Cameron answered. 'You were in a race toward the gallows.'

'I know this!' Renaldo said earnestly, leaning forward, his hands tightly clasped. His brown eyes were entreating. 'Should I tell Lucia all of this?'

'No,' Cameron replied. 'It doesn't seem necessary to me. You've told her enough. She already knows you've been riding a hard trail and now want to quit. Why tell her all of the details? Tell them to a priest sometime if you feel the need to confess.'

'What will you tell the sheriff?' Renaldo asked as Cameron rose.

'I can't see the point in telling him anything, can you?'

'He saw me come into the barn.'

'He doesn't know who you are. It will probably be all right.'

'I wonder. . . .' Renaldo's thought trailed off. 'Do you think any men could be riding on this night?'

'Not unless they're crazy, wildly angry or ignorant. Why do you ask?'

'I did not tell you about the other men – especially the one called Tinker,' Renaldo said. 'I think he is crazy and quite dangerous.'

'Perry Tinker?' Cameron asked, suddenly alert.

'Yes, that is his name. I saw him shoot down two innocent men in Alamogordo.'

'It's not beyond him,' Cameron said. 'Renaldo, you did pick some bad men to ride with.'

'You talk like you know Tinker?'

'I have known him,' Cameron said darkly. 'I think you and Lucia should clear out as soon as the storm lifts.'

'She hesitates to leave – she says you need a cook and it is a blot on her honor if she leaves you now.'

'The heck with that,' Cameron said decisively.

'Becky can cook, maybe not so well, but she can cook. Virginia has been known to boil up a pot of beans. If it comes down to it, *I* can cook camp-fire chow. You two had better plan on pulling out at the first opportunity.'

Which did not appear to be coming any time soon. Slipping out through the barn doors, Cameron saw, or rather felt, that the sandstorm was not going to break for some time yet. And Cameron *had* seen men ride on through storms like this, even resorting to tying dampened bandannas over the nostrils of their horses to keep them from suffocating. If Tinker was that determined to find Renaldo, he was one man who was savvy enough to do it.

Blindly, Cameron made his way back toward the way station, his only guide a flickering lantern in one of the windows, no doubt left burning there by Virginia to show him the way. She had lived through a few of these sense-confusing storms.

Fighting his way through the door of the station which had been blocked with towels, Cameron let in a gust of hot wind and a cloud of dust before he could slam it closed again. Two cots had been set up in the dining room. On one of these sat Sheriff Link Beaton, smoking a pipe. His eyes continued to study Cameron with curiosity, as they had since his arrival. On the opposite side of the room the burr-headed blond man, who had never introduced himself, lifted his head and looked at Cameron with malevolence, perhaps still resenting Cameron's having protected Becky from him that evening.

Dusting off as well as he could, Cameron passed quickly through the dining area to the back of the station where he and Virginia lived. She was waiting for him, wearing a dark-blue silky sort of wrapper over her night clothes, her gray-streaked dark hair loose around her shoulders.

Looking up, she asked. 'Is everything all right out there?'

'It depends on what you mean by all right,' he answered. He walked to the open closet. 'Where's my "necessary-bag", Ginnie?'

'Under the bed,' Virginia answered, noticing that Cameron was holding his injured left arm as if something had happened to it. He got to hands and knees and dragged a small leather satchel from beneath the bed. As Victoria watched with narrowed, uneasy eyes, Cameron walked to a chair, leaned down and opened the satchel. The first item to appear was a can of gun oil, the next was his belt with its twin Colts riding in worn holsters. One of the pistols, the left, was designed to ride

67

butt-forward for a cross-draw, since Cameron Black could no longer draw and fire with his left hand. Certainly not as well as he could when he was a young, cocksure, swaggering gunman back in the days when Virginia had first met him.

Virginia's concern deepened as she watched Cameron partly disassemble his two pistols and begin cleaning them. Outside the storm raged. The lantern flickered.

'Oh, Cam! What's come up to make you break out your guns?'

As he worked he told her briefly of Lucia's and Renaldo's troubles, of which she had already formed her vague surmises. 'Beyond that, there's the big man who wants to take Becky away by force, and Sheriff Beaton. Why he's here, I couldn't guess. And there's the small matter of Perry Tinker.'

'I don't know about him, do I?'

'It might have been after we split up. He used to ride with Big Jim Ramsey and that crowd. He's pretty much a stone-cold killer.'

'Is he quick?'

'Quick enough,' Cameron answered, slapping the cylinder of his reloaded Colt shut.

'When we moved way out here, I had hoped. . . .' Virginia began.

'I hoped, too,' he said, closing the cylinder of the other pistol before he placed both back in their holsters. Cameron smiled faintly. 'It just goes to show that hope is not enough to base your plans on.'

'But we continue to hope,' Virginia said,

'We continue. There's nothing else that can be done,' Cameron answered, rising to blow out the lantern before making his way to their bed.

When Cameron and Virginia rose in the morning the sandstorm was still blowing. This was unusual, but not unheard of. Their usual duration was between ten and twelve hours, but when the wind off the mountains, called 'devil winds', blew fiercely they could last much longer. With no low-growing vegetation on the desert to hold the sand, the winds would continue to shift the soil for as long as it blew.

Frowning at the darkness outside their window which now showed a thin coating of sand on the sill, Cameron lit a lantern. The air felt thick and heavy in his lungs; at this moment he wondered what had possessed him to drag Virginia out to this remote location.

Virginia had risen now, swinging her long bare legs to the side of the bed as she watched Cameron step into his jeans, stamp his boots on and then flip his gunbelt around his waist, buckling it on, in familiar movements.

'I thought the storm would blow itself out overnight,' Virginia said.

'It hasn't. It's a shame – I wanted to clear some of these people out of the station. Now it looks as if we're stuck with them for a while.'

'It can't be helped,' Virginia said with calm acceptance as she watched Cam position his twin Colts in their holsters. 'I never thought you'd have to wear those again,' she said.

'Maybe I don't have to,' he said with distant hopefulness, 'but it seems there's a lot going on around us, and I don't understand it all.'

When Cameron went out into the dining room the two men there were asleep, or half-asleep, on their cots. The sheriff seemed to open one eye and study Cameron in passing. He would have noticed the guns Cam was wearing. The girls, of course, were already up; Cameron could hear sounds of movement in the kitchen as they worked on making breakfast for the travelers. The stage driver, Jennings, and his shotgun rider, the man called Harvey, were still asleep in the back room held for the stage crews. The older woman, Mrs Birch, had been given Becky Grant's room and the

70

two younger women had been forced to bunk together, although they did not complain about circumstances. Cameron was hoping that Becky had told Lucia something about her situation and the burr-headed blond man who seemed to believe that he owned her.

He walked into the kitchen, listening to the keening wind outside, noticing that the two young women were working by lantern-light. He had interrupted something, for he had heard a series of giggles just as he approached the door. Well, young girls have their secrets.

'Good morning, Mr Black,' Lucia said, although, with her accent when she said his name it sounded like 'Meester a-Black.'

'I just came for two cups of coffee – I hope some is boiling. Virginia has a hard time getting started without it.'

'Of course,' Lucia said. Her eyes were bright on this dark, strangely stormy morning. Her thoughts must have been with Renaldo. Becky, meanwhile, was filling two heavy ceramic mugs with steaming coffee. She approached him, noticing his guns for the first time. She said nothing about them. But in a hushed, hurried voice, she did say as she handed Cam the cups:

'Lucia has told me that she will be leaving, Mr

71

Black. Then can I stay here? You'll need a cook, won't you?'

'I'll have to talk to Virginia first,' he replied, seeing her smile fade a little. 'Don't worry about a thing, though. You don't have to go anywhere you don't want to. We'll talk later, all right?'

'Yes, thank you,' she said, her smile brightening again. 'Augie – that's his name – Augie Traylor is not a nice man.'

'The big man out there?'

'Of course,' Becky said.

'We'll have to talk about it later. Come and see me and Virginia in the office.'

'I will – as soon as I can!' she said breathlessly, hopefully.

'Better take a pot of coffee out to the dining area, Lucia,' Cameron Black said. 'People are starting to stir.' He added, 'It's probably not a good idea for Becky to serve this morning.'

'I understand,' Lucia said cheerfully. 'Later, when the men come in—'

'We'll see that Renaldo has his breakfast,' Cameron said, anticipating her request. Renaldo was, after all, her primary focus on this morning; the hope of her life.

After delivering a mug of hot black coffee to Virginia, who was still dressing, fixing her hair,

72

Cameron returned to the dining area. Sheriff Link Beaton had folded his blankets neatly on his cot and was pulling on his boots. Augie Traylor – if that was his name – had done nothing to make his bed, but was sitting up eyeing Cameron with habitual belligerence.

Cameron sat at one of the long plank tables. After a minute the front door was shouldered open and slammed shut again, announcing the arrival of Whitey and Archie Tate. Both were sleep-clouded and dust-covered.

'Good morning, Archie,' Cameron tried.

'Maybe for you!' the bearded hostler said. 'Who can sleep with the wind blowing through every chink, shrieking like a banshee? With cattle bawling.'

'I'll see to the cattle later,' Cameron said. 'I couldn't leave them outside, you know.'

'I think they kept my horses awake!' Archie, whose whole life was centered around his horses, complained.

'There was no choice, Archie. It's happened before.'

'I didn't like it much then, either. Damnable wind – when is it going to stop?'

'When is it?' a female voice demanded. This was Mrs Birch, looking none the better for her rough night's sleep in what she must have considered primitive conditions. 'I mean, when can we travel on? I have people waiting for me.'

The stage driver, Jennings, muttered audibly: 'Lady, among the things we cannot control is the weather.'

Sheriff Beaton, who held a cup of coffee poured from the pot Lucia had delivered to their table, now sat down facing Cameron and asked, 'Seriously, when can we expect relief from the storm?'

'I don't control the weather either,' Cameron said. 'This is already a longer sandstorm than I've seen. It should break soon. I hope so.'

'So do I,' the sheriff mumbled. Then he added: 'I've got you pegged now – it's the way you wear your guns.'

'I don't understand you,' Cameron replied with a faint shrug. He stared into his coffee cup.

'I think you do. Cameron Black, the Arizona gunfighter.'

'Are you going to arrest me – or try to?' Cameron asked in a cold voice.

'For what?'

'How would I know? That's the first thought that crosses a man's mind when he sees a silver star and hears his name spoken.'

'I've nothing on you,' Beaton said frankly. He added as Virginia entered the room in her blue dress, 'And it seems to me that you've given up the outlaw trail.'

'I have,' Cameron assured him. 'Though I never was an outlaw.'

'Just a hired gun,' Beaton said.

'Just a hired gun; too old to hire out now.'

Virginia slid in beside Cameron on the bench, ending the conversation. Lucia served breakfast, which was pretty poor on this morning: cornbread which seemed to be dry, the last of their potatoes which were burned around the edges and sliced too thick, venison steaks. Cameron liked venison, but not for breakfast. He was going to have to slaughter one of the steers, he expected.

Virginia poked at her food, her usually good appetite having deserted her. 'I guess we're going to have to get used to this,' she said. 'When Lucia goes.'

'You see Becky's hand in this?'

'Don't you?' Virginia asked, pushing her plate away.

'I guess I do. But she's doing the best she can. Where do you suppose Lucia was when this was being cooked? Or should I bother to ask?'

'I got up just before dawn and saw her walking

75

back from the barn through the dust of the storm, so you take your best guess.'

'What are we going to do about this mess?' Cameron asked.

'As much as we are doing about the weather,' Virginia answered. 'I'll tell you, though, this makes me wish that I had taken some time along the way to learn to cook myself.'

After breakfast they went into the office with another cup of coffee and went over the books again – provisions were low. Venison was fine, beef was fine, but there had to be something to go with it. Virginia, in the early days in Borrego, had tried starting a vegetable garden, but the sandy soil and arid desert heat had finally made her give it up. Every essential had to be brought up from Santa Fe. Nothing flourished on the long, sere desert; if it had there would have been a population on it centuries ago.

'How about some carrots. . . ?' Cameron was asking. Just then Becky slipped into the room, her blue eyes as wide and frightened as ever. She plopped into one of the wooden chairs and sat trembling for a minute. Finally she told them:

'Augie hasn't given it up. He burst into the kitchen and told me he was taking me away with him as soon as the sandstorm clears.'

76

'No, he isn't,' Virginia said quietly. 'Now, why don't you tell us what started all of this?'

'My uncle Lyle,' Becky began, 'I was forced to go and live with him after my parents were . . . killed.'

'Go on,' Virginia said in the same calming voice, as the wind outside rattled the window. Lantern-light streaked the girl's face with shifting shadows.

'My uncle needed some horses, advertised for them and this . . . man, this Augie Traylor agreed to sell him a small herd. Then Augie said that he wanted me as a part of the deal.'

'Wanted you – that's primitive,' Virginia exclaimed.

Cameron pointed out: 'It's still a primitive country out here, with a large shortage of women.'

'But still! Her own uncle.'

'Uncle Lyle pointed out that I wasn't really con-tributing anything around the ranch. That I was a burden, anyway, and he had a chance to build his ranch up into something. If he could get Augie Traylor to agree to the sale.'

Becky went on: 'Uncle Lyle said that I was going to have to marry someone someday, anyway. Why not take this chance to marry a rich man – which Traylor is. But he is also. . . .' Then, briefly Becky buried her face in her hands. When she raised her tear-streaked face she pled, 'Please let me stay here! I will work very hard.'

'You're staying here for the time being,' Cameron said firmly, without bothering to exchange even a glance with Virginia. He knew his wife: Augie's plan would not be tolerated.

Nothing was visible through the roil and swirl of the dark dust storm. Perry Tinker would not slow down, nor veer toward shelter. Beside him rode Duane Pembroke and Satchel Rose, their kerchiefs over their mouths and nostrils. Tinker was on a mission for God: a mission for which he would be rewarded $50,000. Those who lost would be cowering in their holes in this weather. Those who won would be willing to dare this ride through a heated hell.

The young Renaldo del Campo did not strike Tinker as a man who was willing to brave the savage elements. He would be found in his hiding-place and forced to fork over the $50,000 or go to shooting.

FIVE

Cameron found Lucia at work, scrubbing pots in the kitchen. 'You'd better take Renaldo his breakfast,' he told her. 'It's good practice for being a wife.'

'You and Virginia have been so good to us,' Lucia said, removing her apron. 'And you have no idea who Renaldo even is.'

'I have a fair idea,' Cameron answered, 'but none of it is any business of mine.'

Lucia still watched him gratefully until he turned and strode out into the dining area. Then she got to work, filling a plate for Renaldo. Cameron passed Sheriff Beaton and Augie Traylor, lingering over their coffee, there being nothing else for them to do on this terrible morning. After Cameron had forced open the door and made his way out into the dust storm, Augie asked the sheriff:

'Just who is that man?'

'Him? That's Cameron Black.'

'Cameron Black! I heard that he was dead,' Traylor said, recognizing the name.

'I guess the word hasn't reached him yet,' the sheriff answered, then fell silent. He had no more liking for the abrasive Augie Traylor than anyone else did.

Cameron heard a small chopping sound across the yard even above the whine and wail of the wind. He walked toward the woodpile to find Whitey vigorously chopping wood under these impossible conditions. Gently he touched Whitey's shoulder and shouted to the kid:

'This is not a wood day, Whitey!'

'No?' Whitey looked puzzled.

'No. That was yesterday. Today is a cattle day.'

'Oh. All right!' Whitey shouted back. He buried the head of his axe in the chopping block and followed Cameron along as he led the way through the brown wash of sand toward the barn.

They reached the barn doors about the same time as Lucia arrived with a tray wrapped in a towel to keep the sand out of the food. Renaldo's breakfast. Her dark hair was wildly disordered by the wind, and when the two men appeared from out of the storm, her eyes flashed briefly with fear.

'I did not recognize you at first,' Lucia said. 'I had my eyes closed against the sand. At first all I saw was two shadowy men – I did not know who you were.'

'You're just getting a little jittery,' Cameron told her. 'The sandstorm has something to do with that. It can be unnerving, disorienting.' And the young woman was preparing to launch into a new life, one about which nothing could be predicted, though she must have had many pleasant dreams of how it might be.

Renaldo appeared from the deep shadows of the barn's far corner, his hair somehow neatly combed. Cameron sent Whitey away with orders to feed and water the four steers, then to curry the stage horses if he had time.

Renaldo stepped toward them and took the tray from Lucia, kissing her almost shyly although Cameron was certain that they had spent at least a part of last night together. Lucia paused, looked from one man to the other, then said, 'I must get back to work,' and scurried away, holding her skirts high. Renaldo found a perch on a hay bale and began to eat, making a surprised face at the taste of the food.

81

'That isn't Lucia's cooking,' Cameron Black said, propping one boot up on the hay bale.

'I did not think so . . . is this what I am condemning you to?'

'It fills the stomach. But food is not important at the moment.'

'No,' Renaldo said with a stony expression. He placed the half-eaten tray of food aside.

'What's troubling you, Renaldo?'

'It is the storm. You said that a man would have to be crazy or wildly angry to ride through this sandstorm. We both know such a man.'

'Perry Tinker, you mean?'

'Exactly. He has now had a day to catch up with me. With every hour he could be nearer.'

'He can't track you, not in this weather. How would he know where you are?' Cameron asked.

'I told him, all of them, about Lucia being in Borrego, about my intentions.'

'I see.' Cameron nodded, frowning now. 'Why is he so wildly angry, Renaldo?'

'They think I have the fifty thousand dollars. The money we took from the Alamogordo bank.'

'Why would they think that?'

'Because the money never reached Overton. I believe now it was supposed to be with a courier on the stagecoach . . . the one that I tried to hold up along the way.' Renaldo looked ashamed, disgusted, regretful at once. 'I thought about this most of the night – that must be what happened. They had discussed giving the money to a half-brother of Frank Belavia to transport.'

'Belavia is still around, then?' Cameron asked, for he knew Frank Belavia's reputation as well from the old days.

'Oh, yes. They were all in Overton, waiting for the shipment. I did not realize until later that it must be coming on the stagecoach and some of my friends and I tried to rob it. It did not go well. . . .' Renaldo said. He reached for his tray, then let it drop from his fingers. He had no appetite.

'I don't like this,' Cameron said.

'And I! I may have brought trouble down on you, all of you – and on Lucia.'

'This half-brother of Frank Belavia's, did you get his name, can you tell me what he looked like? He must have passed through Borrego.'

'No one mentioned his name, and I never saw the man, of course,' Renaldo said, shaking his head heavily. 'What am I to do, Mr Black?'

'We have to hope that Tinker didn't take up the trail in this weather or that he was delayed by it along the way. Otherwise, unless the storm breaks this morning so that you and Lucia can ride off, we're going to have to be prepared to fort up and fight it out.'

'I don't know how many men Tinker might have riding with him.'

'No, but you're here. I'm here. Sheriff Beaton is a fighting man. Then there's this Augie Traylor. He's an obnoxious sort, but not the cowardly type, I don't think. We have the stage crew, though I'd hate to get them involved in this. And there's Whitey and Archie. They're hardly gunfighters, but they can pull a trigger. We have a sizable bunch of defenders, really.'

Renaldo still looked miserable. 'I have brought this down on all of you – some of these men might be killed.'

'Save your guilt and your apologies for later,' Cameron told him. 'What we have to do right now is figure out some way to hold Tinker back. And, unfortunately not only do we not know how many men he has with him, but we will be unlikely to even see or hear them coming through the storm. They'll just appear like dust phantoms.'

'What should we do?' Renaldo asked, placing his trust in the more experienced hands of Cameron Black.

'The first thing I have to do is inform Sheriff Beaton that we might be expecting company. In some way that doesn't implicate you.'

'It might be that Tinker is the man the sheriff is hunting for. It was he who shot down two men in Alamogordo. Someone might have recognized him or known his horse.'

'I won't mention Tinker by name. And remember, Renaldo, if Tinker is arrested he is likely to name you as an accomplice. It seems he has no liking for you.'

Renaldo briefly covered his face with his hands. 'Curse this sand blizzard. If not for it, I would be riding homeward with Lucia at my side!'

'And Tinker on your heels with no help at hand,' Cameron reminded him. 'We'll ride this out – the storm and Tinker's attack, if that is what he has in mind.'

Renaldo started to express his gratitude, but when he removed his hands from his face, Cameron Black was no longer anywhere to be seen, there was only a lingering trail of slowly settling dust through the barn doors. He had gone off, presumably for his meeting with Sheriff Link Beaton.

Renaldo had never felt so desolate in his short life. He was only grateful that he and Lucia had shared last night before the end of all things.

*

Sheriff Beaton was alone at one of the plank tables, drinking yet another cup of coffee. He lifted his eyes as the front door opened and Cameron Black accompanied by a gust of wind, a blast of sand and the eerie shriek of the wailing wind entered the way station. The former gunfighter walked directly to the table, pulled down his bandanna and sat facing the lawman.

'We might have a situation brewing,' Cameron Black said, folding his forearms on the table. The sheriff didn't answer, but his eyes narrowed. Cameron went on. 'One of my men thinks that there is a good chance that a band of raiders means to hit the way station soon.'

'For what reason?' Beaton asked reasonably.

'We're not sure,' Cameron said. 'Maybe to waylay a stage, maybe they just want our horses.'

'I see,' Beaton said, a little dubious now. Cameron knew he should tell all that he knew if he meant to enlist the sheriff's aid, but that would be risking Renaldo's freedom, and he wasn't willing to do that. The young man had tried a life of crime and now seemed determined to go straight. Let him ride away with Lucia to try starting a new life. But he knew that a lawman might not view things that way.

'Exactly who is it that is supposed to be riding in?'

Cameron hesitated just a little too long. He saw suspicion growing in Beaton's eyes. The man was no fool. 'He didn't seem to know,' Cameron answered. Quickly he went on, 'But I thought we should all be prepared for the possibility.'

Beaton's face had grown stony, his eyes had gone cold. He knew he was being told a half-truth at best.

'I try to always be ready for any possibility,' he said quietly, but meaningfully.

'Yes, well. . . .' Cameron for once was at a loss for words. 'I'd better go into the office and talk to my wife now.' He rose and started that way, the constant moaning of the wind continuing its tormenting sounds around the station, across the long desert. Already, Cameron had noticed, there were dunes of sand accumulating in the yard. Nature would not be denied. Men could fight the battle to reclaim the land forever, probably only to lose it again.

'Well?' Virginia asked, looking up from the record books she was poring over by lantern-light, 'What progress?'

'I'm afraid we might be losing ground,' Cameron said wearily, planting himself in one of the wooden chairs, and he proceeded to tell her what he had learned and what he had guessed.

87

She studied his dust-streaked face and, amazingly, smiled. 'It will be all right, Cam. We've been through worse than this, remember?'

'I remember, sure. But we were younger then and more – what's the word I want?'

'Resilient?'

'That'll do,' Cameron said, trying the word on for size, finding that it fit well enough. 'The thing is, Ginnie, this place was meant to be our refuge from those terrible times. It seems nothing can ever be left behind.'

'Maybe nothing is meant to be left behind . . . you were saying, carrots?'

'What? When was that?'

'Yesterday, I think. You were asking if we shouldn't have some carrots carted in.'

'We could feed them to your quail,' Cameron said a little sourly. 'I'm sorry, Ginnie – yesterday seems so far away.'

'So does tomorrow, but we have to plan for it,' Virginia said in that reasonable tone which both irritated and calmed him.

'Carrots, then,' he said rising. Though how the owners of the stage line who couldn't even be depended on to provide beef might condescend to ship vegetables overland stumped him. 'I suppose they'll think we should be raising our own in this

Eden if we want them.'

'Quit grumbling, will you?' Virginia suggested. 'No one forced us to take this job.' She smiled as she reminded him of that, softening her criticism.

'No,' he admitted, rising from his chair. He kissed her forehead and said, 'I'll leave you to your wifely duties.'

'I thought I took care of those last night.'

'You did.' He hesitated and asked her, 'Will you do me a favor, Ginnie: keep a gun close at hand? I have no idea how this is going to play out.'

She slid open the desk drawer and showed him her neat little .36 Russian revolver. 'I'm way ahead of you.'

'You usually are,' Cameron admitted. Then he went out to see to the business of running the station.

They expected no stagecoach on this day, neither east- nor westbound. No experienced stage driver would subject himself or his team to travel under these conditions. But those conditions might do little to deter Perry Tinker if he believed that Renaldo was holding $50,000.

Tinker had never liked Cameron Black either. They had faced off once in Las Cruces, but Tinker had backed down under some pretext, and he would take their next meeting as a call to redeem his honor – if and when he saw Cameron. Peering out the window, Cameron saw no signs of clearing; only the waves of drifting, wind-driven sand darkening the desert skies. Nothing moved across the land, man or beast. But Tinker was part both.

Cameron Black had the strong feeling that he was going to have to do what he never wanted to do again – he was going to have to kill a man.

He entered the kitchen just to have something to do – outside work was impossible on this day. Entering, he found Lucia crumpled on the floor, the back door wide open, sand drifting through the room. He first closed the door then crouched to lift Lucia's head. There was discoloration on her forehead. She had been struck.

Lucia's eyes flickered open and she gripped Cameron's shirt front with one hand.

'He took her, Señor Black!' she said in a weak voice.

'Take it easy. Who took who?'

'That man, that Augie Traylor – he took Becky away.'

'How, why?' Cameron glanced toward the darkened kitchen window.

'He said he had made a bargain and she was going to keep it. I was-a. . . .' her voice faltered.

Cameron helped her to her feet. 'I tried to hit him with a frying pan, but he turned and hit me.'

'God,' Cameron muttered, lowering Lucia into the kitchen chair where her shoulders began to tremble as she clasped her hands together between her knees. 'I'll call Virginia. You might be more badly hurt than you think.'

'What will you do, Señor Black?' Lucia asked.

'What do you think? I'm going after them.'

'How can you find anyone out there – in this weather?' she asked, waving a hand toward the window.

'That's probably why Traylor chose to make his move now. I don't know, maybe I haven't a chance at finding Becky, but I am going to try.'

'You can't, Cam!' Virginia said when he told her of his intention.

'How can I not? She was here under our protection.'

'Because . . .' Virginia said a little wildly, 'it's crazy!'

'I know it is,' he answered, then suddenly he grinned. 'But it's far from the craziest thing I've ever done in my life.'

'Bring her back, Cam – if you can – but make sure you bring yourself back,' Virginia said, going to tiptoes to kiss him.

'See to Lucia,' he growled without meaning any offense by his tone.

Cameron struggled back toward the barn. He had not bothered to pause to get his hat. There was no point in it, in this weather. It was bound to blow off along the desert trail. Assuming he could even find a trail to follow.

A madman riding toward the station; a crazy man riding away from it.

It was going to be a day.

SIX

'I will ride with you,' Renaldo volunteered as Cameron Black saddled his six-year-old gray horse.

'No, you won't,' Cameron said firmly. Renaldo's shirt was off and he could see where someone – Lucia, most likely – had tweezed shotgun pellets from his shoulder and then painted the wounds with iodine. 'You're in no shape, besides you may be needed more here, if Tinker is riding to Borrego.'

Cameron filled two half-gallon canteens from the water barrel and looped them onto the pommel of his saddle. The horse was already eyeing him with mistrust. His owner had been known to ride him into uncomfortable, dangerous situations.

Cameron stroked the gray's sleek neck, soothing

it only slightly. He did not wish to take the horse out into this weather, but there was no choice. None at all. The woman-hungry Augie Traylor had abducted Becky in a way that was no less than slavery or an act of piracy. Cameron owed the little blonde an attempt at rescue.

As Renaldo watched, ready to shut the barn doors behind him, Cameron walked his horse outside and swung aboard. The winds continued to howl, pelting him with driven sand. The horse shied at first, not liking this a bit, then lowered its head and trudged forward.

Cameron had no clear idea of where he was going, but if Augie Traylor had originally meant to meet Becky's stagecoach at Overton, that seemed the logical place for the blond man to be headed. What his final destination might be was anyone's guess. It was almost impossible to see the trail, but Cameron Black had been long on this stretch of desert, and he knew it better than most. The only other advantage Cameron had was that Augie had taken only one horse – and that one a stage horse hardly broken to saddle, as an anguished Archie Tate's rapid count had confirmed. The gray that Cameron rode was not fast, but they had ridden many a long trail together, and besides, speed was not called for under these conditions.

Cameron would catch up with the man – unless he had guessed wrong and Traylor was now miles away, riding in the opposite direction.

He did not think that was the case, simply because Augie was not a desert man and would head for a place known to him. An hour on, seeing nothing but sand and more sand drifting in clouds, darkening the land, Cameron drew up his tortured horse and swung down to swab the dust from the faithful animal's nostrils with his bandanna and water from the canteens. The gray's eyes must have been stinging from the pelting sand as well, but there was little to be done for it. He loved that horse, but a small woman's entire future was at stake.

After letting the horse lower its head and try to catch its breath in a breathless land, Cameron started forward again, looking for any landmark, trying to follow the obscured trail. He would have sworn he knew it well, but like a man disoriented in a snowstorm, he was fearful that he had lost his way.

What about Augie Traylor? How could he, who knew little of the stage trail, have found his way? There was the possibility that the well-trained coach horse knew the way, but it seemed more likely that Traylor had simply veered off the road into the desert wilderness. If so, he had doomed himself – and Becky Grant. Cameron felt like hurrying his gray horse on, but that was pointless in the turbulent sandstorm. How much time had passed? How far behind Traylor was he? Had he himself wandered off the coach road? He rode on as the weary, hot hours passed, his horse's head hanging, his own drooping.

Hours, years, eons later he lifted his eyes to the burning sky and noticed something that did not belong there. Among the confused brown cloud cover something silver glinted dully. How could that be?

Then he recognized it for what it was – a star shining magically through the bleak sky, like an answered prayer. He did not dare hope, but then he noticed that the wind had lessened, and another star and then a third appeared. There was a hazy dull glow in the eastern sky. The moon! The storm had broken.

The blown sand began to settle and the skies to brighten. Cameron swung down to see to his horse once more. 'I think we've beaten it, you old gray devil,' he said. Stars continued to flicker on rapidly in the sky as if competing for attention. The dust storm sagged and fell like an exhausted beast soughing to its death, leaving Cameron alone on a limitless, swiftly cooling desert.

All of which brought him no closer to the object of his search.

Where was Becky Grant?

As he stood stroking his horse's muzzle, he surveyed the land as well as was possible by starlight and the dim light of the coming moon. He began to recognize features of the landscape, like emerging images of a puzzle. He could see the uplands where Eagle Pass lay, the town of Overton beyond. Trail-sense or blind luck had brought him this far.

Had Traylor had that kind of luck, or was he out wandering on the desert with Becky?

There was no sense in going back and searching every possibility. That would be a futile excursion. All he could do was ride on, reach Overton and wait for Traylor. With the night now clear, perhaps the man would find his own way west. That was all that could be done. See to his horse, eat, and await the big-shouldered young man who had stolen away a little woman. That was all . . . except to ride on through the depths of the night and wonder what was to happen at the Borrego way station after he had ridden off so cavalierly. Cameron tried to console himself by remembering that there were still a number of armed men back there to protect the station.

And Virginia.

If anything happened to her, Perry Tinker would not have to worry about waiting for the hangman. He wouldn't live long enough for them to string him up. Jaw clenched tightly, wondering about his own sanity, Cameron Black made his steady way toward Overton.

'Can we ride now?' Lucia wondered as she stood next to Renaldo outside the kitchen, studying the clear skies. 'Can we go home? It has been so long.'

Renaldo del Campo did not know what answer the girl really wanted to hear, but there was only one answer he could give her:

'Can we desert these people who have tried only to help us?' He turned her to face him. 'This is the moment we have both been waiting for, Lucia, yet it would be a shame we would have to carry forever if we rode away from their problems now.'

'I know it,' Lucia said miserably, burying her face again Renaldo's chest. 'I shouldn't have even asked.'

'It's what we both want – to ride away from this place, from danger, and to start a new life, but honor demands that we remain. Honor is every-thing to me,' Renaldo said.

'I know it is, or I would not love you. It means much to me as well. So,' she sighed, 'let us try to get past this one last barrier to our happiness – together.'

He kissed her and then turned her moon-bright face up. 'I know who has caused all of this, you see?'

'This Perry Tinker?'

'No, Lucia, this man Renaldo del Campo who thought you could not love him unless he returned to the pueblo with his saddle-bags filled with money.'

'That Renaldo was a fool,' Lucia said with a hint of a smile, running her finger over his lips.

'Yes,' he agreed. 'Sometimes it takes a man long to understand that.'

Lucia drew away, her body stiffening. 'Do I hear horses arriving?' she asked, her eyes wide. Renaldo heard nothing for the moment, but he told her sternly:

'Get inside the station; tell the sheriff and the Señora Black that there may be trouble approaching.'

By the time Cameron made it to the outskirts of Overton the moon was riding high in a clear, cool sky. He judged it to be close to midnight. He had passed not a single other traveler on the road, and he was beginning to wonder if his pursuit of Traylor had been a great miscalculation. His horse was unsteady under him from the long, tiring effort and when he briefly halted the animal it wobbled in its tracks.

He walked it along Overton's streets, where no man was to be seen. In one saloon, he could see lights and hear the usual sounds of men making fools of themselves. Finding a stable at last he swung down and led his weary horse in.

'Hey!' he called out, seeing no one around.

'Hey yourself,' a grumpy voice answered. A scarecrow-thin man straggled out of some back room and walked toward Cameron Black. 'You another one of these men who has no more sense than to ride through the dust-storm?' he demanded truculently.

Cameron ignored his manner. 'Has someone else ridden in?'

'Yes,' the man drawled as if it were none of Cameron's affair. Probably the stableman had been looking forward to a quiet night uninterrupted by travelers, the weather being so bad.

'What did he look like?'

'I don't deal in descriptions, friend, just horses.'

'Did he have a woman with him?' Cameron

asked, persisting.

'I didn't see one.' The stablehand led the gray away, complaining under his breath about the way some people misused their animals. Cameron walked the length of the stable, and there he found it.

It was a company bay, all right. It wore their brand. It looked exhausted, but the stableman had brushed and curried it. Cameron started toward the door; he expected no more help from the narrow man who tended the horses. Was there any law in this town? And did he want to involve them in this? Since Sheriff Beaton had shown up, Cameron's old wariness of the law had returned. After all, he was not positively sure that there were no existing warrants out on him.

There was a long-ridden, sometimes savage trail behind him. That, he decided was the reason he was anxious to see Renaldo set on the right track – for his own sake, for Lucia's. When Cameron and Virginia had finally been reunited, he had been on the run himself with a bounty on his head. Renaldo was still young; he and Lucia deserved better than a life like that.

Cameron Black crossed first to the hotel he had seen. There was no wind at all, he noticed, and it was eerie in its own way to have everything so still after the past few days. The saloon with its muffled, boozy sounds was the only centre of activity in the darkness of midnight. Cameron entered the hotel, finding it lighted, if only dimly, behind closed shades.

He crossed the desk, his silver spurs clinking against the oaken floor.

'Yes?' the woman behind the counter asked. She was blowzy with hennaed hair, pouched eyes and an utterly bored expression. Cameron wondered idly if she were one of the broken-down saloon girls you met now and then; another person who had decided to make her last stand in this hotel. She studied the tall man with the dusty black hair and hard eyes for a long minute before adding, 'What can I do for you?'

'I'm looking for a girl,' he said, and the woman turned that over in her mind, wondering how to take the remark. 'She has been kidnapped and is being held against her will.'

'Are you the law?' the woman asked.

'Family,' Cameron answered, stretching the point. He then went on to describe Becky Grant and Augie Traylor as well as he could.

'She might be here,' the woman said. 'But we don't want any shooting or fights in this hotel. This is a respectable business.'

102

'I will do my best to keep the peace,' Cameron said. 'But the girl has family waiting for her to return safely home.' He tried his best smile, 'I'm sure you can understand how a young woman feels.'

The henna-haired woman, who had not been young for a long time, and had possibly been given up on by her family decades ago, answered Cameron's smile with one of her own, which might have been coquettish many years earlier. She again turned matters over in her mind, finally sighed and said:

'Room Twelve – upstairs.'

'Have you got a spare key?'

'We're not supposed to give those out to anyone.'

'I know, but this is very urgent.' Cam tried his smile again. Before he had allowed it to fade from his face, the clerk slipped a master key across the counter and Cameron palmed it. 'Family honor,' he said for no particular reason, then turned toward the staircase opposite the counter.

His spurs continued to chink against the floor, but he did not pause to remove them. Even if heard, they could belong to anyone, and who would believe that anyone would have been crazy enough to pursue a man across the desert in that wicked weather? Maybe Augie Traylor did not know how crazy Cameron Black was.

Black mounted to the uncarpeted landing and made his cautious way to Room Twelve. He heard no sounds beyond the door. No light showed through under the door. He inserted the key as silently as possible and swung it wide, drawing his right-hand Colt as he did.

Becky Grant who had been having a nightmarish dream composed mostly of suffocating winds and wild beasts, heard the small snick of the key and sat up in bed, holding her blankets in front of her, prepared to scream, fight or run – whichever seemed most likely to allow her to escape from the brutal hands of Augie Traylor. Instead when the door was cautiously toed open, she recognized a form which could only be one man.

'Mr Black!' she said, managing to shriek and whisper at the same time.

'It's me. Where is he?'

'I don't know. I was so exhausted, too tired to move really. He locked me in here, and there's no escape but the window, and it's two floors to the ground below. I couldn't jump without breaking a leg, I don't think. I believe he would have gone somewhere to get liquor, don't you?'

'I don't know his drinking habits,' Cameron said. 'It's likely, I suppose. Get dressed; I'm taking you out of here.'

'What if he comes back?'

'Then I'll have to break my promise to the lady behind the desk. I'll shoot the miserable bastard down.'

'I didn't think you talked that strongly.'

'I've been seriously provoked. Get dressed, lady,' Cameron said roughly, trying to prod her into motion.

Then what? He hadn't any money in his jeans to hire two horses, and Becky could not have any – even if the obstinate stable owner agreed to let them rent them. His own gray could not run any more on this night. Well – one step at a time.

Traylor had still not returned as Becky was pulling on her boots. Perhaps he had gone off to get tanked up, to celebrate his victory and to prime himself for what he believed to be a romantic evening to come. Beyond the window of the hotel room, the silver moon glowed brightly. Cameron had looked out of the window as Becky dressed, and determined that as Becky had said, there was no good escape route that way. He mentally urged the girl on to speed.

When at last she was finished – does no woman

at any time ever dress quickly, no matter the circumstances? – he opened the door again, and with
caution stepped out into the hallway, his Colt held
loosely in his right hand.

And nearly bumped into Kyle Melrose.

The stagecoach driver pulled up abruptly in his
stride and croaked, 'Mr Black!'

'It's me, all right, Kyle – what are you doing
here?'

'The dust storm hit; I had to halt my team. Now
it's cleared and I have to take the road east. I'm
carrying a valuable cargo – bearer bonds, actually
– and they have to get through to Santa Fe or some
business deal or other is going to fall through. It's
clear now. What I still don't have, and do need, is
a shotgun rider, and I haven't been able to find a
volunteer.'

'You've got one now,' Cameron Black said. 'I've
one more passenger for you,' he added as Becky
appeared, shivering, in the doorway. 'Except, we
can't pay the fare.'

'You're both company employees, aren't you?'
Melrose said. 'You're entitled to free passage to
wherever you're going. Borrego Springs, I
assume.'

'That's right. We're going home.'

Melrose didn't ask them what they were doing in

Overton, what their relationship was – with their both having emerged from the same hotel room. Kyle was only concerned with the job at hand. 'As soon as I get my team hitched by that silly s.o.b. at the stable, we'll be on our way.'

'Have you got an express gun?' Cameron asked with some concern.

'Poor old Van McCoy's ten-gauge. This should be an easy run, even in the dark, once we get through Eagle Pass. Even outlaws had enough sense to hole up today. They won't be expecting a midnight stage.'

'No,' Cameron agreed. The coach line had rules against running at night. Even the best driver could lose his way; even the best horses could break a leg against an unseen obstacle, leaving passengers or valuable goods stranded on the desert. But there were always exceptions. This, it seemed, was one. Melrose had been told that this run was urgent.

'If we're going,' Melrose said, 'let's get cracking. I don't want to be out on the flats if the storm starts to blow again.'

'Do you think that could happen?' Becky whispered. She took Cameron's arm and they started downstairs. 'That the storm could rise again, I mean?'

'It seems unlikely,' he answered, looking across the empty lobby. There was no sign of Augie Traylor. It seemed that Becky had linked the sandstorm and Traylor in her mind. He did not know which she feared the most. But she continued to cling tightly to his arm as they crossed the lobby, Cameron Black leaving the key on the counter, and went out into the brittle-clear, cool night.

'We must be lost,' Duane Pembroke said from behind his bandanna mask. He thought that the storm must have disoriented them and they were now riding out on to empty desert.

'We're not lost,' Perry Tinker snapped. 'This is the old coach road. I've traveled it many times.'

Pembroke grumbled an answer. Satchel Rose, who had not spoken more than two sentences through the stormy night, said nothing, just kept his weary horse plodding along through the drifted sand. How they were supposed to run on these horses even if they were ultimately success-ful, he could not guess. His roan faltered again and he pulled up.

'My horse has had it!' he said angrily.

'There will be fresh ponies at the station,' Tinker said, circling back.

'And a coach and sweet-potato pie,' Rose said sourly.

'Nobody forced you to come,' Tinker said savagely.

The sandstorm had begun to clear and now Pembroke lifted a pointing finger and called out, 'I see a light! That's got to be Borrego Springs. There's nothing else out here.'

'Swing down, let the horses blow for a while,' Tinker ordered. 'When the moon rises, we're starting down. Don't start getting angry with me, boys – there's fifty thousand dollars ahead on the trail.'

At least Tinker believed there must be. If Renaldo had taken the money and ridden off to retrieve his woman at Borrego, the young man had likely been caught there by the dust storm. He would still be there waiting it out. And when Tinker caught up with him, Renaldo would either cough up the money or pay a terrible price in blood.

SEVEN

The stage rumbled on through the close shoulders of the bluffs of Eagle Pass. They were making good time, even in the darkness of midnight. They had a rising moon to help show them the way, and both driver and team knew the trail well. Kyle Melrose drove intently, on the alert for any obstacle ahead. Cameron Black sat watching every shadow for possible attackers, but as Kyle had said, even the outlaws had had sense enough to hole up during the storm, and they expected no trouble.

Becky Grant sat miserably inside the coach, wondering what would become of her now. Mostly she just hoped to get far enough away from Augie Traylor that he would realize that further pursuit was useless.

They reached the downgrade not half an hour

on, but even with the sudden clarity of the night, Cameron's searching eyes could not spot a light from the Borrego station. It was too far distant, he knew, but the sight of a lantern burning would have comforted him in some way.

Tinker? They had not passed him, and so Cameron had to assume that the outlaw was still intent on raiding Borrego. Cameron again had to wonder if he had made the right decision in pursuing Becky, although that had been successful. But it had taken long hours.

He knew that Renaldo was still at the way station, together with Sheriff Beaton, Whitey and Archie Tate, Jennings, the stage driver from the east and his man, Harvey. They should be enough to hold back any raid by Perry Tinker and his outlaws. The thought did little to comfort him. Cameron had no idea how he could continue on if anything were to happen to Virginia, and he silently urged the team of horses to quickness down the mountain grade.

Tinker waited a full hour and then another, letting the night pass. He wanted those at the way station to be asleep or lulled to inattention by the passing hours. In that time the three outlaws had not seen anyone moving. There had been a light in the barn, but that had been extinguished, leaving only a faint lantern glow at the rear of the house, which, from the iron stovepipe piercing the roof, Tinker took for a kitchen.

'How many you think are down there?' Duane Pembroke asked with some restlessness and some uneasiness.

'The manager of the place – probably he has a wife. A hostler and maybe a yardman for chores,' Tinker answered.

'And Renaldo.'

'And Renaldo,' Tinker agreed. 'His woman, he told us, was the cook, and there was someone moving around in the kitchen. That makes four men with guns. The station master is probably some crippled-up old driver or maybe a retired soldier. None of them is likely to be sleeping with guns near at hand – there hasn't been any Indian trouble around here for a long time.'

'Renaldo is the one to worry about,' Rose said.

'I've seen the kid with a gun – he's not much good,' Tinker said.

'Maybe not, but you can bet he'll be sleeping with a weapon at his side.'

'What do you want to do, Tinker?' a steadily more anxious Duane Pembroke asked.

'Wait until all the lights go out. The one we see

112

is probably just the girl finishing cleaning up in the kitchen. Then we'll start down. Nobody jumps out of bed in the middle of the night prepared for a gunfight. We have all the advantage, boys.'

The way they determined to do it was for one man to take the barn – they knew from the earlier lantern light that at least one man was in there. Hostlers normally slept close to their horses, so that was probably who it was. Renaldo, they guessed, would be in his woman's room – that was where Tinker would be if it were him. Tinker himself meant to take the front door of the way station; he ordered Rose to take the kitchen door. They would sweep in, probably find an old way station manager in his night shirt, possibly his wife, find the girl's bedroom and yank Renaldo out of there, put a gun to his head – and the girl's if necessary – and demand that he give up the stolen $50,000.

Tinker was confident that the plan was a good one. He could not know how many holes there were in his theory. The problem was that Tinker thought deeply but not well; he had forgotten that this was the reason he had given over the planning of operations to Frank Belavia. Belavia was a slow-thinking, slow-moving man, but his plans were always meticulously thought out. Nothing was left

113

to chance or to sudden impulse.

Tinker didn't know that he could have used Belavia at that moment. But then he didn't intend for Frank Belavia to ever see a cent of the stolen bank loot.

The three outlaws, intent on their raid, started down the long slope toward Borrego.

The stagecoach had broken from the mountain trail and reached flat ground once again. Although it was dark and there was drifted sand across the road, Kyle Melrose whipped his horses and urged them on. He had been promised a bonus if the bearer-bonds he was carrying reached Santa Fe on time ... and threatened with being fired if they did not, the weather notwithstanding. The businessmen in Santa Fe were not concerned with the weather or troubles along the trail, but only with getting their funds on time.

Cameron Black tried to relax. There was nothing he could do, and he knew that Melrose was making the best time he possibly could under the circumstances, but it was not good enough. His station, *his Virginia*, were threatened, and he felt a vague sense of guilt and a strong sense of urgency. He caught himself sitting hunched forward in the coach box, straining his eyes against the night,

hoping for a first glimpse of the poorly constructed adobe house he now called home – the
only one he had had in many years.

Duane Pembroke approached the barn cautiously.
The bandits had decided to walk the last fifty yards
or so, leaving their weary horses ground-hitched in
a clump of creosote bushes. Rose and Pembroke
both had misgivings about escaping on their
horses, desert-dry and now near foundering, but
Tinker had insisted that there would be fresh
horses at the way station; after all, a large part of
their function was to provide fresh horses for the
stagecoaches. If these weren't as well saddle-
broken as they would like, well that was too bad –
they would be mounted and on their way out of
the territory at least, with no one to pursue them.
Not out here.

The other two exchanged glances, but were
forced to agree. There was really no other choice;
besides, Tinker had provided them with an
income, no matter how precarious, for a number
of years now. When had they robbed a bank or
held up a stage without some element of danger?
Never.

Now Pembroke was next to the barn, one hand
on its heated siding, the other holding his Colt

revolver. The timing of this was important – Tinker wanted Pembroke to enter the barn first and silence anyone within before he and Rose booted open the way station doors. Pembroke hesitated. Perspiration trickled into his eyes and he cuffed it away. Just for a moment he thought he heard, distantly, the sound of an approaching coach. But after midnight? Following the dust storm? He shook that notion aside and crept toward the barn doors. Parting the double doors he wedged himself in between them. The first thing that happened in the gloom of darkness was that he came nearly face to face with a cantankerous steer that lowered its head and made threatening gestures with its horns.

A cattle barn? That made no sense. Pembroke eased around the steer and started down the row of stalls facing the walkway. True to Tinker's prediction a dozen horses stood there, watching him with faint light glimmering in their eyes. One of these backed away at his approach and then whickered.

That set off a response from the other horses who neighed in a surprised chorus and even started the cattle to bawling. A voice boomed out of the darkness, and a man Pembroke could not see in the murky barn demanded:

'Who's there?'

'Just shut up and back away,' Pembroke barked, now seeing Archie Tate's shadowy form in the corner of the barn. 'Or I'll just have to gun you down.'

'I give you the same advice,' a voice from the loft said and Renaldo added, 'I have you in my sights, Pembroke.'

'del Campo?' Duane Pembroke said shakily, letting his eyes shift upward.

'That's right. If I were you, I'd put that gun down.'

Pembroke debated internally, then in a desperate move he flung himself to one side and from his back fired three times into the loft. His pistol bucked in his hand, his gun's roar was terrific in the barn's close confines. Fire spewed from its muzzle and a cloud of black powder smoke clotted the air.

Something jerked at his sleeve. Something crushed his chest. He thought that one of the steers had stepped on him as they twisted and turned away in panic. But it was nothing of the sort. Touching his chest he found a spurting flow of hot blood pumping from his shirt front. He cursed Tinker and his crazy plans, the gun fell from his fingers and he died on the manure-stained floor of the barn.

Renaldo came down from the loft, taking three rungs at a time. Those shots would likely open the gates of hell – for Perry Tinker was out there somewhere, and he would not be deprived.

'See to him,' Renaldo shouted at Archie Tate as he raced toward the doors.

Archie Tate already knew that there was nothing left to be seen to, but he agreed.

Renaldo's only thought was Lucia, and he rushed across the yard even as he heard the uproar in the way station begin.

Sheriff Link Beaton was awakened in the cool of the midnight hour by a shoulder being slammed against the back door of the station, by the crack of wood and the creak of iron hinges. He rose from his bed, grabbing for his holstered pistol which hung at the head of his bed.

He fumbled in the darkness, unable to locate his revolver in the unfamiliar surroundings, then finally located it and stepped out into the hallway to find Satchel Rose in the dark kitchen.

'Whoever you are. . . .' Sheriff Beaton began in a solemn warning, but Rose already had his gun in his hand, and he was not waiting to find out what the man in front of him had to say. He triggered off twice before Link Beaton had the time to answer his shots. Beaton's training as a lawman had always taught him to issue a warning before he went to shooting, but this time his training let him down. One of Rose's bullets banged into a copper kettle hanging on the wall behind Beaton, the second passed through the sheriff's leg, dropping him to the floor.

Renaldo, bursting through the front door which Tinker had already opened, heard the sound of a kettle rattling in the kitchen, and his first thought was of Lucia. He raced down the hallway, his heart thudding. He passed the old woman, Mrs Birch, who was emerging from her room with her wrapper held tightly around her throat, shouldered past her without apology and rushed into the kitchen, not knowing what to expect.

What he came upon was not what he had imagined, but Satchel Rose standing over Sheriff Beaton who lay writhing on the kitchen floor, bleeding heavily from a leg wound. Rose looked as if he intended to finish the job as he stood over Beaton with his gun in his hand,

'*Hombre*!' Renaldo shouted out, and when Rose shifted his eyes and the muzzle of his gun towards him, Renaldo shot him dead.

Link Beaton continued to clutch his damaged leg. He murmured something that might have been a plea for help, might have been his thanks, but Renaldo did not remain in the room. He had to find Lucia!

Running back down the hall, he found Mrs Birch still in her doorway. He shouted: 'There is a man who needs help back there!' not knowing if the woman was capable of helping. The house was still dark, and Renaldo, who had never been this far into the interior of the place, made two false turns, cursing his luck.

Virginia had awakened when the shots sounded from the barn. She rose, removed her .36 revolver from its hiding place and braced herself resolutely for whatever was to come.

Tinker had been prowling the dark interior hallway. He, too had heard the shots from the barn, and figured that Pembroke had taken care of any opposition there. Then there were heavy gunshots from the kitchen, and he decided that Rose had capably taken care of whoever that might have been. Tinker continued to make a series of poor assumptions, but he was a confident man and believed that he and his plans could not fail.

Approaching the door on his right, he paused and listened. He could detect the scent of a woman's powder and soap. He smiled thinly –

Renaldo's woman. And Renaldo was likely hiding in the bedroom as well. He prepared to make a cautious entry, gun held level.

When Perry Tinker kicked the door open he found himself facing a dark-haird woman wearing a dark-blue wrapper. There was a chrome pistol in her hand.

'Who are you?' Virginia demanded, although she thought she already knew.

'Well,' Tinker said, looking appreciatively at the tall woman, her dark hair loose across her shoulders. 'You're not the way I imagined you, but I can see how Renaldo would have been attracted to you.'

'Renaldo. . . .' Virginia half-laughed, but before she could explain further, Perry Tinker took a step forward and drove the barrel of his Colt down on Virginia's wrist. Her gun clattered free to the floor and Tinker took another step toward her, eyes glinting.

In the distance Virginia thought that she could hear the sound of a team of horses approaching, but she gave that thought up as imagination. Perry Tinker had something definite in mind, and whatever it was, it was not going to be pretty.

EIGHT

Perry Tinker resembled a wolf in the moonlight that filtered through the window of Virginia's room. He had shoved her roughly back on the bed and he now hovered over her, his eyes demanding. Virginia thought that she had seen rougher men in her time, but not for a long while. Now she had Cameron Black to keep them away – except that Cam was not here on this confusing night!

'I'll keep this simple,' Tinker said, 'I'm here for the money. Where is Renaldo?'

'I don't know,' Virginia said honestly. She was cradling her injured wrist on her lap.

'I didn't expect you to say anything else,' Tinker said in a sly voice. Tinker was one of those men you run across who think they are sly when they really understand nothing going on around them.

Now he tried what he assumed was a reasonable tone. 'I don't even want to hurt Renaldo. I really don't. He was a good soldier for me . . . until this last betrayal. I just want the money? Do you know where it is, little lady?'

'No, I don't,' Virginia answered.

'Then get up!' Tinker said savagely. 'You're going with me. I'll trade you back to Renaldo if he decides to be reasonable.' Tinker paused thoughtfully. 'Write him a note. Tell him the terms – his sweetheart for the money.'

Virginia rose and reluctantly crossed the room to her desk. She thought of trying to disabuse Tinker of the notion that she was Renaldo's woman, but thought he would not believe her: his mind was made up. Even if she could convince him, what then? He would take Lucia, and Virginia thought herself more prepared by life to survive an abduction than the young girl. Painfully, her wrist swelling now, she scribbled out a note:

Renaldo, dear,
Tinker has me and will not let me return to your
loving arms unless you return the stolen money to
him.

Tinker glanced at the note and was satisfied with

it. 'All right,' he said, propping it up near the lamp. 'That's all I can do for now – let's get riding.' Virginia reached for her dress, but Tinker stopped her. 'That's a waste of time, besides you might not be needing any clothes again if Renaldo doesn't come through.' There was no mistaking the quiet menace in his voice.

'I don't think he has it,' Virginia answered.

'Let him tell me that,' Tinker said. 'And he will tell me something once he finds out his woman is missing. Come on, let's get going.'

With that Virginia was taken out into the hallway and then to the dining area.

The westbound stage driver, Jennings and Harvey had appeared in the hallway, and with his pistol Tinker waved them away. Virginia also made a small gesture to the men. There was no need for them to get involved in this.

Stepping out into the cool of the night, Tinker looked around, still expecting Rose and Pembroke to rejoin him. He stood there irresolutely for a few minutes, his gun fixed on Virginia who had begun to shiver beneath her flimsy wrapper. Then he heard the unmistakable sounds of a coach arriving from the west, trace chains clinking, horses clopping, a brake being applied. It was still some distance off – Virginia knew that the experienced drivers slowed their teams well ahead of the station. But her eyes flickered that way.

'A midnight stage?' Tinker said with surprise.

'It's probably my husband,' Virginia said. 'He would come through the night.'

'Your husband?' Perry Tinker stared down at Virginia. 'What do you mean? I thought you were Renaldo's woman.'

'You might have thought it. I never said it.'

'What's your name, then?' he demanded.

'Virginia Black.'

'Black?' Tinker looked truly puzzled. He had been certain. . . . 'What's your husband's name?' he asked as the coach drew nearer.

'Same as mine – Black. Cameron Black.'

'Cameron. . . .' Tinker reacted like a man stunned. 'Come on, woman – I don't know if I believe you or not, but we're leaving.'

Virginia couldn't tell whether the approach of the stage, the thought that she was lying and was actually Renaldo's woman, or a fear of Cameron Black now spurred Perry Tinker into motion, but he took her by her injured wrist and yanked her after him, walking out onto the desert where the bandits had tethered their horses in the clump of creosote brush. Virginia was shoeless and the going was rough, yet Tinker didn't allow her to slow. He continued to yank on her injured wrist as he dragged her forward. By now, she knew, the stage had drawn up at the way station. She did not really know if Cameron could have found a way to return on the coach. The idea seemed far-fetched suddenly. Maybe he was still out there, lost on the desert, or more likely, sleeping in the Overton Hotel. She could only wish that he had somehow made it back.

Because if he had, Perry Tinker had a whole lot more to worry about than she did.

Tinker, his mouth set in a frown, continued to lead her on. They must have gone half a mile now, and still there was no sign of the horses. Perry was thinking: What if the stupid animals had scented water and hay ahead and broken their tethers. Alternately he thought about the woman's words. *Cameron Black?* How could that old-time gunslinger find himself stuck out in this lonely desert outpost?

He had thought that Black had been killed years ago, had heard that he was badly crippled-up. Then Tinker thought, as he trudged across the desert, towing the woman after him: maybe she had told him the truth. If so, perhaps Cameron Black was young Renaldo's boss, the brains behind the scheme to double-cross Tinker and Frank Belavia and steal the Alamogordo bank money.

126

Tinker liked that possibility better. It explained why Black might be staying out at the wretched desert way station. Black would know what the stages were carrying and could pass the word to Renaldo and his gang of insiders – probably including that crazy trio, Carlos, Sabato and Fuego. That made more sense than anything else.

And it cheered Tinker somewhat. If he had made a mistake and grabbed the wrong woman, which now seemed likely, why, he had the wife of the gang leader hostage! Cameron Black himself would turn over the money for his wife, would he not?

Tinker had a healthy respect for Cameron Black. Years ago when Tinker was still riding with Big Jim Ramsey the two had faced off in a little border cantina. Tinker had still been young and had felt the need to show off in front of his men. He picked the wrong man. Cameron Black, wearing his twin Colts low, had turned away from the bar and raked Tinker with his eyes. Tinker knew that he had made a mistake, then someone had whispered the man's name to Perry. At that time in Arizona Territory there were few with Cameron Black's rep-utation, and Tinker had backed off saying something about it all having been a mistake. He might have lost some face in Big Jim's gang, but no one could blame him, and on occasion Tinker knew that he had made the right decision.

But that was then. Now, by all accounts Black was nearly a cripple. They said that he could no longer even shoot with his left-hand gun. That was at least fifty per cent better odds.

They came upon the horses.

Two of them had broken their tethers and wandered off looking for forage, but Tinker's own mount was still there, and Satchel Rose's roan, and that was all he needed at the moment.

'Climb aboard, lady,' Tinker commanded. 'I figure you can ride astraddle.' There was a hint of innuendo in Tinker's words, but Virginia was too cold, weary and experienced to take offense at childish humor. Besides, her feet hurt. Placing a bare foot into the stirrup of the roan, she swung into the saddle, noting that the horse was shivering, not from cold, but from sheer exhaustion.

'This pony's not in shape to ride far,' she said.

'We're not going far – or fast. We just need to draw Renaldo out. Or Cameron Black if he really is here.'

'He really is,' Virginia assured him, not knowing if Cam was or not. 'Or he will find you eventually, so it makes no difference. He will ride you down, Tinker.'

Tinker's voice seemed to quaver a little, but he answered: 'I'm not afraid of a crippled-up old man.'

'Who've you been talking to?' Virginia challenged Tinker. 'I see him every day and he's in the same shape he was in ten years ago. Take my word for it, or ignore it at your own risk.'

'Shut up,' Tinker said as he swung into leather. His confidence was beginning to develop cracks. He snatched the reins from Virginia's hands and started leading her out on to the long, cold, featureless desert.

'Well,' Archie Tate said as Cameron stepped to the ground from the coach box. 'All hell has broken loose here. And where were you when it happened?'

It was then that Becky Grant stepped out of the coach and approached them timidly. Archie Tate eyed her with some unhappiness. The girl had caused a lot of problems.

'What has happened, Archie?' Cameron asked.

'A man dead in the barn and . . . you go on inside, maybe the others had better tell you the rest.' Archie glanced at Kyle Melrose then and said disapprovingly to the driver, 'Did you have to run this team half to death!' He smoothed a hand

129

along the foam-flecked flank of the lead horse. Kyle declined to answer the hostler.

'See to the team, Archie,' was Cameron's order as he stepped up on to the way station's porch and went inside, his anxiety growing with each stride.

The first sight he saw was Sheriff Link Beaton seated in one of their two stuffed leather chairs, his foot propped up on a foot cushion, his trousers off, while the elderly Mrs Birch tended to a wound on his thigh. Then Renaldo, still bare-chested, emerged from the hallway, his arm draped around Lucia's shoulder. The girl looked unsteady, terribly frightened.

'Why don't you boil us some coffee, Lucia?' Cameron asked. 'If no one else could use it, I could.'

'There's a dead man in the kitchen, Señor Black,' Renaldo said.

'He was trying to kill me,' Sheriff Beaton said. 'Renaldo here saved my butt.'

'All right,' Cameron said, rubbing his forehead. 'I'll see to it later. I have to talk to Virginia first.'

'She's gone,' Jennings, had to tell him. The stage driver came forward. 'He had a gun on us, and Virginia motioned us not to try anything.'

'*Who* had a gun?' Cameron shouted. 'Where is she?'

'We don't know,' Renaldo answered. 'Jennings and Harvey described the man to me. I think it must have been Perry Tinker who took her. She left a note,' he said, offering it to Cameron who scanned it quickly.

'*Why* . . . never mind,' Cameron said, the word spitting from his lips. Why did not matter. 'Did anyone see which way they went?'

Heads were shaking negatively, but Whitey, who had crept into the room, said, 'I seen them going west. They were walking. The man said something about having horses out there.'

Cameron used one of his rarely used wide assortment of curses and turned to face Sheriff Beaton. 'I need a fresh horse. Can I borrow your buckskin, Sheriff?'

'Go ahead.' The sheriff winced as Mrs Birch did something to his wound. 'It doesn't look like I'll be needing it for a while.' His eyes softened: 'Good luck to you, Black.'

'Do you want me along?' Renaldo volunteered.

Cameron looked at the wounded man, at the trepidation in Lucia's eyes and replied: 'Thanks, but no. I take care of my own business.'

Sheriff Link Beaton's buckskin was a deep-chested, well-mannered mount. Although a little stubby, it was quicker than Cameron would have supposed. He had no doubt that he could run Tinker down – if he could find their trail in the darkness of night, the hoof prints in the soft sand of the desert floor.

But Cameron had several small advantages. Whitey had given him a fairly good idea of their starting point. The moon was still riding high. And the earlier wind had left a virtually virginal carpet of untrodden sand across the desert.

Cameron smiled despite himself when he found the tracks of two horses riding eastward, the prints deep and obvious.

Why eastward? Why any particular direction at all? Only to put some distance between Tinker and any pursuer. He had nowhere to run, but if he meant to recover the stolen money – which, as far as Cameron knew, did not even exist, unless Renaldo was a better liar than Black took him for – Tinker would have to stay near the way station. The man was not fleeing, but trying to set a trap. He would have to negotiate or go to guns.

Cameron favored the second option.

Besides, he had nothing to negotiate with.

The tracks wound on across the trackless desert, leading nowhere. They wandered south and then west, then east again. Cameron was being led into the wilderness, and he knew it. He had several

132

thoughts: he could try to trick Tinker into believing that he knew where the money was and strike up a false bargain – but trickery was not his strength, and he did not think that Tinker would fall for a flimsily constructed tale. Alternatively, he could ride the man down with guns blazing – which was his style. Except that Tinker had Virginia with him. Cameron would not risk letting her be injured or killed in a gunfight.

That seemed to allow only for stealth and wary caution, so Cameron rode on silently. There was nothing stirring on the vast desert. Moon shadows gathered beneath the tall spiny ocotillo plants and at the bases of the occasional weary stands of greasewood and patches of nopal cactus he passed. It was like riding across some deserted moonscape. Not a man, not a coyote, not a lizard appeared for what seemed like hours but was less than scattered minutes, as Cameron could judge by continuously glancing at the descending moon. There was a rising breeze now, dry and warm, and Cameron wondered if he had been wrong in assuming the dust storm was truly dead, never to return. If conditions like those of the past few days arose, this would prove to be an exercise in futility.

And what would that mean to Virginia? He heeled the buckskin on to greater speed.

He could tell by the sign he was following that the horses he was tracking were faltering, beginning to slow badly. Their strides were shorter and now and then he could identify a dragging track that indicated a horse had briefly stumbled. It was no wonder, if Tinker had hurried them through all the way from Overton and then forced them to continue without so much as a drink of water. Such treatment of the horses would have brought a flood of excoriation from Archie Tate's throat, but Cameron only smiled grimly. His prey could not last much longer on the desert. Tinker – one way or the other – was nearly done.

Cameron tried to penetrate Tinker's way of thinking, but could not. Tinker had been called mad, perhaps he was. What did that bode for Virginia?

Cameron Black halted the buckskin on the crest of a sandy rise. He could see them now: two plodding horses, casting crooked moon-shadows across the flats. He knew that he could ride them down at that moment, but he was hesitant. If only Virginia could break away from the man! But she could not, not aboard an equally weary horse with Tinker certainly holding a gun on her. A decision had to be made and quickly.

134

Ahead on the desert flats was a low, brushy arroyo. If Tinker kept on his present course, he would have to approach it. The buckskin shuddered beneath Cameron. It, too, was growing weary, but it had been well-rested and seen to by Archie Tate over the past few days. Cameron did not know what he could say to Sheriff Beaton if he ran his horse to death. But that was nothing when weighed against Virginia's safety, so, as he retreated down the rise and pointed the buckskin southward, Cameron did something he seldom did, he applied his spurs to the horse and sent it into a full gallop toward the arroyo.

At a dead run the buckskin still was not a fleet animal, but it was certainly quicker than the horses Cameron was pursuing. They came upon the arroyo half a mile later; Cameron slowed the buckskin and turned its head northward to follow the gravel-strewn bottom. Rain fell once or twice a year out here on the average, but when it did it flooded the channel, so there were a few straggly survivors along its course – dry, gray willow brush, a seemingly dead cottonwood tree. There was no water in the arroyo, of course – only slippery stone and quartz gravel, which shimmered like diamonds in the moonlight. The horse's hoofs made too much noise across this dry creek bottom to suit

Cameron, but there was no cure for that.

He had already made his plan, and he meant to follow it through.

The bluffs along the arroyo were nearly at head height for a mounted man, but Cameron could not see up and over, which was good in that it meant no one could see him either, but he had to time this properly, to cut Tinker's trail precisely. He drew the tiring buckskin to a halt in the ravine and tried listening, but he heard nothing. Maybe Tinker had decided to change his course again; he had already shown himself to be erratic, unpredictable.

With no enthusiasm for the project, Cameron swung down, ground-hitched the horse and scrambled awkwardly up the sandy bluff bruising elbows and knees as he made his way up the loose soil of the bank. When at last he dared to look up and over the rim he saw the two horses approaching on weary legs not more than a hundred yards away. Slipping, sliding, Cameron went down the slope, returning to where the buckskin horse stood waiting.

Not fifty feet farther on, Cameron found a tongue-shaped ramp where the sandy soil had given way, forming a natural exit from the arroyo. He checked the loads in his Colts although he knew they were both clean and ready. Then he started the buckskin up the ramp.

NINE

The desert was long and empty, utterly soundless when Cameron Black rose out of the arroyo like a dark angel riding. Perry Tinker was too stunned at first even to think of drawing his handgun, and by the time he did it was already too late.

Virginia was a quick-reacting, clever woman. She knew instantly who the dark approaching rider was, knew what he intended, and she flung herself from the saddle to land upon the sand. When Cameron saw that she was temporarily out of danger, he drew his right-hand Colt and fired three times from the back of the hard-charging buckskin horse. He could not tell how many of his shots actually hit Tinker, but at least one certainly did, for the outlaw threw his hands wildly into the air, let out a high-pitched scream and fell from his saddle to the ground, his horse dancing away in confusion.

Cameron circled his horse. He looked first for signs of life from Perry Tinker, but there was none. Then he rode to where Virginia sat against the earth, rubbing her head.

Her hair was in a tangle, her night-robe bunched and open. If she had had a mirror at that time, Virginia would have screamed in embarrassment, but to Cameron Black she had never been more beautiful. Sitting against the white sand, her face moonlit, her beauty struck him anew. She was alive! Warm and confident and loving. This bold woman was his, and his alone. Cameron swung down from the buckskin and went to her.

'Are you all right?' he asked, crouching down beside her.

'Now I am,' Virginia said. Helping her up, Cameron noticed that she winced when he took her wrist, saw even by the pale moonlight that it was badly swollen.

'Did he do that?'

'With his gun barrel. It was my fault. You taught me never to get that close to a man so long as I had the drop on him.'

'He might have shot you otherwise,' Cameron said seriously.

'He was too mad about finding the money. Cam, does it really exist?'

'I don't know. We'll have to talk to Renaldo again about that. Are you ready to ride?'

'No,' Virginia said, rubbing her hip which she had bruised in launching herself from her horse's back, 'but I'm sure ready to go home and tuck into my own bed.'

'I'm sorry, Ginnie,' Cameron said. 'I guess I let you down, taking off like I did.'

She halted and turned toward him in the glow of moonlight. 'Cameron,' she said seriously, 'you could never let me down. Did you find Becky?'

'I found her, brought her back with me on the stage. She wants to stay on for a while.'

'She is still afraid of that man – Augie Traylor.'

'It seems so. We can give her enough time to get over that feeling, I suppose, and send her on her way. Then we'll have to find another cook somehow,' Cameron said as they trudged through the deep sand and collected the horses.

'Oh, well, if we have to, we will – somehow.'

'Yes,' Cameron Black said. He glanced at Perry Tinker's body. 'I thought we had left all of the violence behind us.'

'I suppose it can't be done,' Virginia said. 'There's violence in towns, in the city, on the

140

empty land. It's a shame and a pity, but you can't hide from it, wherever you are.'

'I guess not,' Cameron Black said. Gently he helped Virginia onto the saddle of her horse, mounted the buckskin, caught up the lead to Tinker's weary horse and they started off across the empty miles toward . . . home.

There was a flurry of activity at the way station as they approached, which puzzled Cameron Black. There was a row of five horses in front of the station and lights blazed from every window. He said to Virginia, 'I don't like this.'

'Oh, God,' she only murmured. 'No more shooting!'

'Don't assume the worst,' Cameron said, although he already had, even though he could make no sense of the situation. 'Listen, Virginia, I want you to ride behind the barn and stay there.'

'Cam!' her voice was a low, weary gasp. 'Let's just ride away.'

'No,' he said fumly. 'It's our duty, and it's our home. Someone is violating it, and we can't allow that.'

'That's just your pride talking,' Virginia said.

'All right: it's just my pride.' He leaned far out of the saddle and kissed his wife. 'Now get to the barn

141

and stay out of sight.'

He watched Virginia reluctantly ride away. When she was lost in shadows he swung down and made his way toward the station. He saw Whitey sitting on the front porch, knees drawn up, arms looped around them. The kid was shivering and he stuttered as he pointed a thumb back toward the station and said weakly, 'M-men, beating people up and b-breaking things.'

'All right. Whitey, you'd better scoot toward the barn and find a place to hide out. Virginia is there, you can watch out for her.'

Which probably wasn't true, it was more likely that Virginia would have to watch out for the kid, but it set him into scrambling motion away from the station house.

How did he want to handle this, Cameron wondered. Sneak around and peer into windows, try the back door? No. He was good and angry. His life, his home had been invaded by a pack of men about whom he knew nothing, over money about which he knew nothing. He felt his temper rising. It was not nearly the same as the fury that used to pass through him in his younger days, but it was somehow more intense.

If the gunfighter, Cameron Black, was dead and gone, still his ghost lingered and just now his anger was burning hotly.

Cameron kicked the front door to the way station open.

Sheriff Link Beaton still sat in the corner chair, Mrs Birch crouched beside him as if hiding herself from the world. Jennings and Harvey sat in the opposite corner, hands behind them, obviously bound. Archie Tate stood nearby, angry and confused. Of Renaldo and Lucia there was no sign: perhaps they had made their run for Mexico. Becky Grant sat opposite the door, face in her hands, as if she could take no more from life on the desert. Around them were bunched five men who were strangers to Cameron.

'What's this!' Cameron Black demanded.

'Who the hell are you?' the stocky man who appeared to be the leader of the gang asked as Cameron entered the room.

'The question is – who are you?' Cameron replied, his right hand dangling near his holster. 'If you boys are waiting for a stage, the next one won't arrive until around eight o'clock. But I guess you're not. Passengers don't usually tie up my crews.'

'My name,' the stocky man said, coming forward, 'is Frank Belavia. Are you in charge here?'

'You've put on some pounds, Frank,' Cameron

said. 'And yes, I'm in charge here. You want my name?'

'No,' Belavia said, 'I've got it now. Cameron Black! Long trail behind us.'

'Very long. What in hell are you up to, Frank?'

'I want Perry Tinker.'

'So do I,' Cameron said. 'He made off with the money and my wife!'

'Your wife?'

'He made a mistake, thought she was Renaldo's woman, then he decided to hold her hostage so that I wouldn't try to catch him.'

'What happened?' Belavia said, seemingly sincere.

'I went after him, what do you think? But I couldn't find him, so I guess he's got the money and is heading for Mexico or parts unknown.'

'With your wife? And you let him go?'

'Women come and go,' Cameron shrugged. As he spoke he watched the other four Belavia riders.

'That doesn't sound like the Cameron Black I know,' Frank Belavia said. 'When you were younger, a man wouldn't dare take a toothpick from you.'

'We all mellow, Frank,' Cameron said, attempting a smile. 'Every toothpick's the same as the next, every woman is the same as the last. I would-

144

n't have minded finding that money, but it's not the first big score I've missed out on.'

'Are you still riding the owl-hoot trail, then?' Belavia said, coming near enough that Cameron could smell the trail-sweat on him: a sort of broken-tooth scent.

'When I have the chance. I have a good cover for myself here, Frank. I try to keep up appearances.'

'Clever,' Frank Belavia said, believing that the whole story was a bit too clever. He had known Cameron in the old days, and he had known his attachment to Virginia Scopes, as he had known her himself. There was no way, come hell or high water, that Cameron Black would get off Tinker's trail if Tinker had Black's wife as a hostage. At last he said: 'I don't believe a word of what you're saying, Cameron.'

Cameron had let the man come too close to him, and now he took two steps back, not liking the scowl on Belavia's face. It was five against one, but Cameron saw no other way out – the cavalry was not going to ride in. It was true that he could no longer draw and fire accurately with his left hand, but as he drew his right hand gun he managed to simultaneously flip his left-hand revolver to the wounded Sheriff Beaton.

Cameron shot Frank Belavia in his chest, and the man died in his tracks. Beside Cameron, Beaton triggered off two shots that sent a man dancing drunkenly across the wall before he collapsed in the corner.

From the kitchen, Renaldo, who had more staying power that Cameron had given him credit for, emerged and fanned two rapid shots from his pistol and sent another Belavia man reeling, his Colt flying free. The two remaining outlaws dropped their guns and threw their hands high. They had not hired on for this type of job.

Archie Tate looked around at the fallen men as he gathered the lost guns and said, 'Lord – it's a massacre!'

Augie Traylor decided he had had enough. He stood at the window of his hotel room, watching the eastern sky begin to lighten faintly, and rubbed a hand across his short hair. He had considered riding the long desert again. But he remembered the suffocating heat of the sandstorm, the empty lifeless land. No, he had had enough. Besides, Becky herself had a protector in Cameron Black – a man known far and wide for his prowess with a gun.

She wasn't worth it anyway! She would be hard

to tame, liable to run away at any opportunity. Traylor pulled on his shirt and remembered a girl he had seen in a saloon the night before: a little plump, maybe, but with a nice smile and a ready laugh. She was short, had dark hair and sparkling eyes. Once Augie had told her about his ranch, told her how wealthy he was, she would certainly be willing to marry him. If not, well, he would simply take her. In the long run it would be to her benefit. Augie reached for soap and razor and faced his grinning reflection in the mirror. It would be a good day – let Becky Grant be a drudge, a cook in some lonesome way station if that was what she preferred!

There were plenty of women who would jump at the chance to take care of Augie Taylor.

Morning dawned as if the white sky were made of ice. The flourish of dawn's colors was limited to a single strand of pinkish embellishment when Cameron, wearing his sheepskin coat, stepped out into the morning air. Archie Tate, having risen earlier, was already harnessing the team of horses to their coach for Kyle Melrose's run to Santa Fe. These were breathing steam from their nostrils as Cameron approached through the chill of morning.

'You're a man, Archie,' Cameron said warmly. The hostler only grunted an answer and then began his habitual complaining.

'You've forgotten that we still have Jennings's eastbound stage to outfit. I tell you, there's no end to it!'

Cameron Black, used to Archie's complaining, only smiled. Dawn was cold, noon would bring temperatures in three figures, yet it was a good day.

He had taken his wife to bed last night after the uproar had died down. Frightened by still more shooting, she had rushed to Cameron's waiting arms and they had stood together for a long time without bothering to speak. There was no need for words.

On this morning all was well.

The dead had been dragged from the house and hastily buried. Cameron had spoken to Jennings, the coach driver, and requested that he return Cameron's gray horse from Overton on his next trip east.

'He'll mind the tether well; he's traveled that way before.'

'All right,' Jennings had answered. 'We should have an easy trip of it – it seems like you've pretty much cleaned out that bunch of Eagle Pass raiders

148

without leaving home.'

'I hope so,' Cameron had said. 'Only time will tell.'

There were still the two unnamed Belavia riders to deal with. They had spent the night handcuffed in the kitchen, watched over by Sheriff Beaton. He was transporting them to Santa Fe on the east-bound coach, although he wasn't sure what charges he could actually lay on the men's heads.

About Perry Tinker he was more direct. 'I spent a lot of time pursuing that man – since the Alamogordo hold-up, and here he delivers himself to me! And I wasn't prepared for it,' the lawman said shaking his head. 'Thanks to you, Black, he won't trouble anyone ever again.'

'It wasn't a sense of good citizenship that caused it, Beaton. It was a cold fury about what he might have done with my wife.'

'Be that as it may, you have gotten rid of a bad man no one's been able to catch. He killed two innocent citizens during that bank raid, you know. I'd like to see you get a reward or at least some sort of citation for that.'

Cameron laughed. 'And spoil my bad reputa-tion!'

Becky was in the kitchen preparing breakfast before the travelers left; Virginia had emerged

149

from the bedroom to sit beside Cameron. She had bathed, and her woman-scent was clean and quite intoxicating. From the back of the hall Lucia and Renaldo had appeared to stand, holding hands like the young lovers that they were.

'What about me?' Renaldo suddenly asked.

'What about you? Do you want a citation too?' Link Beaton responded.

'About all of before,' Renaldo said, his accent deepening with stress. 'Don't make a joke of me!'

'I'm not doing anything of the sort,' the sheriff said flatly. He spared Lucia a brief smile and a knowing nod. 'I sometimes have lapses of memory. The first thing I remember about you is when I saw a man standing over me, ready to kill me and you took care of him when I was helpless to defend myself.'

'That is all!' Renaldo asked in disbelief.

'That's all. You need to take that little woman there and get on back home – though I wouldn't recommend you ever returning to Arizona again.'

'We do not intend to,' Lucia said, firmly linking her arm around Renaldo's. 'We have made our plans.'

'Good luck with them, then,' Link Beaton said, then – not with originality, but with heartfelt good wishes – 'and may all of your troubles be little ones.'

150

After the young couple went toward the barn to gather up their horses and ride south, Cameron Black said: 'That was kind of you, Beaton.'

'Oh, what would have been the point in arresting him? There's no proof that he was there anyway. I've eliminated the two ringleaders – or rather you have, Black. Renaldo is young. He made a mistake, but I think he's decided it doesn't profit anyone in the end to ride the outlaw trail.'

'I suppose so. We can only hope,' Cameron answered.

'Isn't that what you decided, Black?'

'I was never an outlaw,' Cameron objected.

'I've seen posters on you, son,' the sheriff said mildly.

'All of that was—'

'Stuff you'd want to spend years in court trying to disprove?' the sheriff asked. Then he rose from his chair and started toward the eastbound stage. Kyle Melrose was still in a hurry to ensure that the bearer-bonds he was carrying were delivered to Santa Fe on time. Simultaneously Jennings clanged on a brass bell he carried on his stage announcing that the westbound stage he was guiding was ready to roll.

Mrs Birch appeared from the back room and strode toward the front door, walking like a pelican. Reaching the threshold, she turned to fix a matronly glare on Virginia and Cameron and announced in a reedy yet firm voice:

'I thank you for your hospitality, but I assure you, I will never utilize this stage line again!'

Then she was gone and Virginia and Cameron shared a laugh before walking out onto the front porch to watch the two stages departing in different directions, each transporting their disparate people with differing tales to tell.

They stood watching until the trails of dust had settled. Then Cameron said quietly. 'Well it's just you an' me alone together again.'

'Not quite,' Virginia said, pushing him away with one hand – she could read her man's eyes well enough. 'You're forgetting about Becky.'

'You're right, I was.'

'What are we to do with her?'

'She said she wanted to stay around for a while. Maybe you could teach her how to cook.'

'Me?' Virginia laughed again. 'My idea of cooking in the old days was to tell the waiter that my steak was overdone. I haven't gotten any better. You?'

Cameron admitted: 'On the range I knew my meat was done when it started to catch fire. Well, maybe she'll get better at cooking. I kinda think she needs us, and right now, we need her as well.'

'I suppose,' Virginia sighed, 'and if we ever wanted her to go – I suppose it would be me who would have to tell her.'

'As per our agreement. . . .'

They said at the same time, 'We each do what we're best at.'

Cameron put his arm around Virginia's waist and they went back into the house, smelling something that seemed to be beans burning.

Later he said to Virginia in the tiny office: 'I guess I'm going to have to butcher one of the steers today. Did our shopping list go out with Melrose on the eastbound?'

'Yes. I made sure of that. When we'll get any supplies is anyone's guess.'

'There's still the quail,' Cameron said, joking.

To his surprise, Virginia opened her desk drawer and removed a small object no larger than his thumb tip.

'What is that?' he asked.

'It's a quail egg, darling. While some of us fritter away our time killing badmen, others find ways to provide. I have a covey of eight birds in a coop out back.'

'I'll be damned,' Cameron said.

'Probably . . . but I'll be beside you no matter

what,' Virginia said, rising to embrace him.

Unexpectedly Becky Grant appeared in the doorway, her hand poised to knock. Virginia disengaged herself from Cameron's eager embrace, patted her hair and said, 'Yes, Becky?'

'I just was wanting to start dinner, but I couldn't remember what time the next stage was due in.'

'Six,' Cameron muttered, his arms falling reluctantly away from Virginia.

'Not until six o'clock, Becky. You've plenty of time,' Virginia told her.

'Oh, good – I'll just clean up a little, then.' She watched the couple without realizing that she had interrupted anything. 'Really, I'm so pleased to stay on here – this is a lucky place,' she enthused.

'Lucky?' Virginia said in bewilderment.

'Yes. Think of it – Lucia found her man, I escaped from one I never wanted, you two are here to watch out for me!' She sighed. 'I only want to stay here in Borrego. And who knows? The next coach through might be carrying a strong, kind man I like.'

'Your beans are burning,' Cameron said and the girl rushed down the kitchen. He said to Virginia: 'This is a lucky place?'

Softly she replied, 'It has been for us, has it not?' and nestled closely into his arms again.

154

'I suppose so. Let's hope that the stage carrying Becky's longed-for man is not too long in coming – I hate burned beans.'

'Oh, you just like to gripe,' Virginia said.

'You know how to put me in a better mood.'

'Quail eggs?' she asked innocently, and he kissed her.

Walking out into the heated sunlight of full day, Cameron watched as Archie Tate, riding his stubborn little pinto pony, trailed in from the west, swung down and stalked to where he stood. Archie reached the trough, took a wooden pail of water from it and doused his head and upper body. Then he shook his head.

'I couldn't find the man, Mr Black. Maybe he wasn't killed after all. Maybe just stunned.'

Cameron's expression was uncertain. He was sure that he had killed Perry Tinker, and had sent Archie out so that they could bury him; no man deserved to be eaten by scavengers and vultures out on the long desert. Maybe his directions to Archie had been inexact.

Or maybe Tinker *was* still alive.

'Thanks for trying, Archie.'

'All in the day's work, besides, the pinto hasn't had any exercise for a long while.'

Wearing a frown, Cameron walked back toward

155

the adobe way station and told Virginia what had happened.

'But he was dead, wasn't he?' she asked.

'I thought so, but he could have been feigning. My main concern was getting you home at the time.'

'Stop worrying, Cameron,' Virginia said lightly. 'Even if he did survive – what would be the point in him coming back to Borrego?'

In the meantime, Whitey made a startling discovery in the woodpile; although he didn't know how important the red carpetbag was when he stumbled across it, others did.

TEN

Whitey didn't know what he was looking at, but it did not belong among his stacked cord of wood. No one had told him what to do on this morning after all of the excitement of the night before, so he had returned to the woodpile. He enjoyed watching his silver-bright axe blade cleaving the white wood of the logs. He could not have said why, but he liked the precision of his sharp implement separating wood from wood, falling into nearly precise segments which he then stacked beneath the dome of the white-blue desert sky. It made Whitey feel that he was alive, participating in the grand scheme of things, rather than only observing its passing.

The red carpetbag seemed to be an intrusive element in the scheme of things as Whitey saw it.

It did not belong where it was! It had invaded his small well-ordered world. Almost angrily – though Whitey was never truly angry – he pulled the bag from beneath the logs and marched it toward the way station.

'I have found something,' he told Cameron. 'Some passenger must have left it.'

Cameron nodded and took the bag from Whitey, who released it as if it were an odious object. In the office, Cameron and Virginia opened the bag and found what it contained: many thousands of dollars.

'It must have been that little man Phillip Kramer, don't you think?' Virginia asked. 'He must have been the courier whom everyone was waiting for.'

'I suppose. I wonder why he left it here?'

'Fear,' Virginia said. 'He didn't want to be blamed for failing, so he meant to tell Tinker or Frank Belavia – whoever – that he had stashed the money in a safe place, and leave the rest up to them.'

'I suppose you're right. . . .' Cameron was saying when the improbable and bizarre figure of Perry Tinker appeared in the doorway to their room.

The man was sand and dust from head to toe, his face streaked with sweat rivulets, like a man who had arisen from some dusty grave. The Colt revolver in his hand, however, seemed as new as the day it had been manufactured. Cameron reached downward, but he had not worn his guns – there had seemed little point to it on this day. From the corner of his eye he saw Virginia slide open the drawer of her desk.

'What is it, Tinker?' Cameron Black asked boldly.

'What do you think it is?' the red-eyed outlaw panted. 'It's on the bed beside you. Fifty thousand dollars of mine!'

'What makes you think it's yours?' Cameron asked, almost pleasantly.

'Because I say it is. Flip the bag over here,' Tinker said, cocking his pistol. Cameron was still watching Virginia's furtive movements.

'You don't know who you're tangling with,' Cameron said.

'An old, crippled gunman without a weapon!' Tinker said, and he laughed, but his voice was as dry as dust.

'No,' Virginia said, 'he means me.' And her little .36 Russian triggered off twice, sending Tinker reeling back against the wall. This time, without pity, they watched him die, and there was no mistaking his final gasps.

'What is it?' Renaldo asked, bursting into the

room with his Colt in hand. Then he saw Tinker, the Remington revolver in Virginia's hand and muttered, '*Madre de Dios.*'

His eyes then fell on the red carpetbag. 'Is that the bank money?'

'Yes.'

'I don't want to touch it – give it back to whoever it belongs to,' he said. 'Enough is enough. I see where all of this leads,' he added, glancing again at the still form of Perry Tinker.

'That's where it leads,' Cameron said softly. 'Take Lucia away from here and build the best life you can for her.'

Renaldo nodded, and without speaking, turned and walked away from them, his boot heels clicking on the floor.

'You did good,' Cameron said as he took his trembling wife into his arms.

'I had to shoot with my left hand,' she replied, holding up her swollen right wrist. 'Cam, I'm turning into a mirror image of you.'

'Darling,' Cameron Black answered as he folded her into his arms, 'you always have been my mirror image. Here we are at the end of our trails, and do you know what? It's as Becky said: this is a lucky place.'